Dedicated to my father,

Donald Samuel Kingery.

He was a mining engineer

dedicated to safety for miners.

Chapter 1

The Tragedy

The bells rang out loudly. Anne caught her breath and counted, Bong, Bong, Bong, Bong. The clanging stopped for 15 seconds and then started again always four blasts. She whipped off her apron. As she turned to run from the house, Shawn appeared his eyes wide set in a pale face. She paused for a second and opened her mouth. Shawn shook his head. "I'll watch 'em Mum – GO. She joined the crowd running to the mine, praying as she ran. Four blasts meant the shaft her husband worked in was affected by whatever had occurred, but everyone came. Some to dig, some to watch, some to pray and those from section 4 to mourn. As they neared the mines, she saw frantic digging. Men waited their turn. Anne searched the crowd and found many of her neighbors breathing heavily dirt covered and some bleeding or unconscious. None of them made eye contact with her. Donald must still be down there. It was for him they dug, for him they prayed and for him they waited. The owner came in her carriage. She didn't get out, but her son did. He ran to the mine and like Anne searched the faces of the dirty exhausted men. When he didn't see Donald, he looked at her. She was standing apart from the others. Her face pale, her eyes dry, staring at the shaft. Sam ran to the shaft, grabbed tools, a helmet and disappeared inside. The woman in the carriage started as though to stop him but instead settled back slowly shaking her head. Her expression didn't bode well for her son when he returned. After the longest five hours of Anne's life, even longer than when she labored to bring their little ones into the world, longer even than when they had labored to clear the rubble off of her Dad's lifeless body when this same mine had buried him eight years ago. That day it was Donald who found him. Her husband of only a year. The shock put her into labor that night and Shawn was born. The woman in the carriage had left after an hour but the carriage returned with only a driver. Two hours later she still stood there. Shawn had brought her James to nurse twice, but she barely noticed. Most of the men were gone now, called away by the insistent bells that rang to call them to work the other three shafts. After another hour men started out of the shaft. In the midst of them was Sam cradling a body whose lines she knew well. As Sam approached, she fell to her knees, arms stretched out to receive his broken frame. Sam gently set him down and the remaining number four shaft miners surrounded her. Each had a word about her beloved, how he had helped or encouraged them. Some reminded her that his broken body was healed now. None of their words made sense to her. They were just sounds. The men brought a plank and four of them hoisted his body upon it and began the trip to the cemetery stopping at the warehouse on the way to pick up one of the ten cheap scrap wood coffins kept there. The owner might pay for burying, but she didn't pay much. He'd be buried right away and out of supposed generosity she 'd have a week to move out of the company house. His last pay would be docked what they owed at the company store. Death benefits would be gathered at the pub that night from those who could ill afford to give. As the men proceeded to the field to dig the women gathered around her. Smart enough to know that speech would fall on deaf ears they helped her up and walked her home to change to the black dress they knew hung in the back of her closet. They knew for they each had one too, waiting for the need to mourn. Anne hugged her children, most too little to understand. She changed to the dress, put black arm bands on each child and from under the bed pulled a thin sheet. Every year she had embroidered part of a picture onto it. It showed a happy family on a picnic

4

by a lake. She had used bright colors of yarn leftover from the sweaters and mittens she made for Christmas every year. She handed the roll of cloth to her neighbor who ran to the burying field. Before her children got there, Donald would be wrapped in it, so they needn't carry the picture of his scraped and bloody body as she did of her Dad and now of her man. The miners weren't used to having Sam among them. He hadn't been home for several years. They were impressed with his willingness and ability to dig and surprised when he found Donald as quickly as he did. Now he helped wrap the body and place it in the coffin beside the hastily dug hole. They stood hat in hands as the women approached. Anne's second youngest peered into the box. "Look Mummy, your picture" she lisped. Shawn took her hand and that of the 6-year-old and pulled them away gravely watching his mother. He was old enough to understand what lay under the picture. He had friends whose fathers had disappeared. They usually left within a few days and he never knew where they went. Once he thought he saw one of them sifting thru rocks, but his Dad had tossed him onto his shoulders and hurried away talking about how people could resemble other people.   The minister, who had traveled in from one town over when he heard of the tragedy spoke of Donald's broken body being healed and suggested he was in a better place. Donald's favorite hymn was sung, and his favorite psalm read. After the man had said his piece and the men filled in the grave everyone quietly stole away taking the children so Anne could grieve alone. Only Sam stayed, and the minister who stayed because Sam stopped him when he started to leave. The minister reached a hand to Sam stopping him when he tried to talk to Anne. "Wait," he counseled. "She won't hear anything now." Bowing his head Sam walked to the carriage and climbed in. Surprised but very grateful to find it empty he endured the ride to the big house. Tears flowed down as he remembered his childhood friend. Even after he turned ten and his mother sent him to boarding school so he couldn't hang around what she called a bad influence and riffraff he had managed to stay in touch. A maid could always be bribed to carry a message and he spent a great deal of time fishing during his vacations but rarely successfully since he usually sent home his catch with his friend. He knew Donald had always shared the fish with Anne's family also. When Donald started working in the mines and told him stories of how dangerous it was down there Sam was horrified. He arranged a tour so his mother wouldn't realize who had told him and then went to her describing the deplorable conditions the miners worked in. His mother heard him out and told him there was nothing that could be done. Mines were dangerous. She then sent him for a year abroad to mature him. Instead of distracting him though he used the time to tour mines overseas. He discovered that mines didn't have to be death traps. That there were safety measures that could be taken to not only avoid cave ins but could make the miners less prone to injury. After six months touring mines in Germany, Poland, and Britain he came back to the states to meet with teachers at Ohio State and other colleges with engineering programs. He checked statistics on mine safety and visited mines with programs in place that made a difference. He wrote home of his ideas for improvement and received short curt notes that his mother was implementing some of his ideas. He arrived home yesterday and was just sitting down to breakfast when the clanging sounded. As he ran for the carriage, praying that no one was trapped, he realized that number four was where his friend worked. They were rarely in touch unless big events happened. He was still in school when Donald married Anne, the girl whose family got most of the fish he had caught. He received four more letters, one when each child was born. The last only six months prior. He often wondered why Donald didn't mention the improvements or answer his questions. Each time he sent a gift and a note back via the closest minister. After washing the mud off and changing his clothes he went looking for his mother. He found her in the library reading. Laying aside her book she proceeded to tell him how inappropriate his actions had been. Men of his stature do not run into mines nor dig graves. He furiously asked why she had lied to him about improving safety precautions in the mines. His mother straightened up and looked down her nose at him, an action which used to strike terror in his heart. This time he merely crossed his arms and stared her down. After a few minutes he told her he was going to take over management of the mines. Drawing back Abigail said, "You can't, they belong to me. Your father left them to me. "Sam left the room and didn't come back into his mother's presence for 2 days. He had all his meals sent up and let her think he was sulking. The morning of the third day Sam again found her in the library. Laying aside her book once again she looked at him. "Well, I hope you're ready to be reasonable now. Sulking for days isn't a mature way to handle a problem but I will forgive you this time." She said magnanimously. Grimacing, Sam said "I talked to the attorney before I left on my last tour. I know Dad left everything to me with the provision that I provide for you. The attorney said it would take a while to transfer things over and we kept in touch while I was traveling. The transfer was completed yesterday. I just received the paperwork. I came home to take over the company." Abigail gasped and yelled, "No you can't, you need me. You know nothing about mining you'll destroy our way of life. I won't allow it I'll get my own attorney." Sam shook his head, "You can try but since you no longer have any funds at your disposal save what I give you I don't think you can hire an attorney. Actually, I have learned a great deal about mining over the last few months and I know how to hire people who know even more. "After a great deal more shouting and complaining, Abigail resorted to whimpering. "I was only trying to do what's best for you. I wanted to build your fortune so you could marry well. I didn't want you to have to resort to grubbing in the dirt the way your father started. "Really Mother? "retorted Sam. "Creating such unsafe conditions that the best friend I ever had died before I could see him. That's what you felt was best for me?" "Yes," she snapped. "and throwing his family out today as well. They'll be gone and you'll never see any of them again. Do you really think the paltry sums you offered the footman made him loyal to you? He is my employee and knows what to do when a family loses their support. He is on his way there now to drop them off in a town far from here so you can't find them again. I don't care what happens to them." Thanking God, he'd started sending gifts and missives through the closest minister instead of the footman Sam ran to the stables and saddled his horse. Vaulting onto the saddle he whipped him into a dead run headed for section four housing. When he got there, he saw the wagon sitting in front of a house. There were boxes piled onto the porch and the footman was arguing with Anne. Sam heard Anne's angry tone, "You said I had until 2 PM and it isn't even noon yet. You have to wait." The footman leaned into Anne and muttered something Sam couldn't hear. From the look on Anne's face it was probably good that he couldn't hear. Sam threw himself off the horse and grabbed the footman by his collar. He threw him down into the dirt and glared at him. "Your services are no longer needed by my family. If you are caught on my property again you will be jailed. I hope you are." Sam turned to Anne who was standing shocked several feet away from him. "Are you ok?" He asked quietly. Anne nodded. "Are you the one who will drive us to a town a few hours away and drop us like so much baggage? " Sam flinched and walked slowly over to her. "No Anne, she didn't send me, and no one is going to drop you off in a town to fend for yourself. I had no idea she had kicked you out and when she told me I grabbed the fastest horse and came over." Anne gestured to the wagon. "That's the unwelcome wagon. It takes widows, their families, and one crate per family member to a town and drops them off in an alley sometimes with our crates, sometimes not. We are left to survive anyway we can or die. Our children end up in the streets, an orphanage, or a small unmarked grave. Now why are you here?" Sam stared at her. "The widows and children are left to starve? Are you serious? " Anne glared at him. "That or become slaves or worse. Now again, before she sends our chauffer back, what do you want? I know you and Donald stayed friends over the years. The gifts you sent may enable me to keep my little ones few a few more months if I can keep the footman from pilfering my money. If you want my thanks for bringing him out, you have that. The men told me you found him, and I am grateful." Anne looked into Sam's eyes and fell silent for a moment. "You didn't know, did you? We were told it was your decision, but it was all her wasn't it? I always wondered how Don could be so loyal to you. I think he knew it was her. He always defended you when the men grumbled." Gathering his courage Sam asked Anne to sit down. He explained what had just transpired between him and his mother. He told her he wanted to change things, but he needed to know what was going on before he could make a difference. Then he reached for her hand and said, "Anne Don was barely alive when I reached him. He

11

looked at me and asked me to take care of you and his little ones. I nodded and he was gone. It took me another hour to free his body. I want to keep that promise Anne. He was my best friend. Please let me keep that promise." Anne looked at him and said," How? I want my babies to live but how can you help. I can't stay here that would be favoritism and the men would grumble. The women would assume the worst and I can't expose my children to that kind of talk. You can't support us somewhere else for the same reason. Rumors are the only form of entertainment here and I don't want to be in one." Sam nodded. "I know I've been over and over so many ideas but only one rings true. Marry me Anne. I can support you then and your little ones." Anne drew back sharply. "There have been widows who remarried to avoid being abandoned in some town but to another miner. You're the owner. No miner would take on four children, they simply couldn't afford it." "I can." Said Sam. "I'll gladly raise Donald's children and any we have as well." Seeing her look of fear, " he added. "You'll need time to mourn, our marriage would be in name only until you say." "And if I never say?" she inquired. Sam looked sad but said." Then I'll only have four children. We'll be partners only." "And your mother?" said Anne, "She'll agree to this? I don't want my children treated badly by her." "She doesn't have to agree." Said Sam. "She is moving out. You need never see her. She won't be a problem. Marry me Anne please right now." As she hesitantly nodded the carriage drove up. The groom jumped down and opened the door. He helped the minister and his wife out. She ran to Anne and hugged her. "Are you ready Anne?" asked the minister. "Let's gather your babies and pray over all of you and then we'll help load this wagon so you can begin your journey. Sam took the minister aside and explained the change in plans while Anne whispered to his wife. "I wondered why your carriage came for us." Said the minister. The footman Sam had thrown out earlier climbed down off the back of the carriage and Sam told him to load the crates into the wagon. He just looked at Sam "Not my job uh Sir, I only drive it. They load and unload." Sam glared at him and the footman hurriedly started loading crates. Glancing at his groom she asked "Why did you bring him? I thought I fired him." "I found him going through things in the stable. I was afraid he was stealing so I told him he should come appeal his case to you. I wanted to keep an eye on him. I'm sorry if that was wrong." No, you did the right thing, thank you" replied Sam. "We'll keep him in line. In fact, when we get back you can help him pack one crate of his belongings and make sure you go through every single thing he

13

puts in his crate. Then put him in the wagon and drop him off at the nearest sheriff's office crate and all. It's more than he did for all those widows these past years." A neighbor herded the four children over to their mother, but Sam stopped her and asked her to watch them a few more minutes. Then he turned to the minister who was conferring with Anne. When they both nodded, he smiled and reached for her hand. A few minutes later he took the baby from the very surprised neighbor and ushered all of them out into the yard. He helped Anne into the carriage and handed her the baby. He walked to the wagon and told the footman to deliver the crates to the big house. The footman started going through the crates, but Sam stopped him. "I have to do my usual inspection to make sure nothing was stolen." He complained. Sam grabbed his collar and threw him into the driver's seat. "Sir" the footman went on we rent these cabins furnished. They get everything but clothes, food and blankets. Almost every time I find a spoon or a cup." Sam turned away and climbed into the carriage after telling his groom to keep the wagon in sight at all times so that there wasn't time to go thru the crates. As they traveled up to the house, he asked Anne if he really owned everything in the houses like the footman said. Anne explained that there was precious little anyone in the sections owned. Amy, the six-year-old piped up. "You look scary, are you mad at us?" Sam started back then picked her up and dangled her on his knee. He saw that April was trying to hide behind her mother and Shawn was putting his hand across her in a protective stance. "No precious, not at you or any of your family. In fact, I'd like you all to be my family now." "Will we live in a different section now?" asked Shawn. "No child, we'll live in my house, only it will be our house." Answered Sam. At that bit of news, the four-year-old burst into tears and started pounding with her fists. "No! No! NO!" she screamed. "I don't want to live there, the witch lives there She'll eat me like Gret'l. She'll hurt us." Once Sam had deciphered what she was screaming about he picked her up and patted her back. He calmed her down by rocking back and forth while murmuring reassuring words. When she was reduced to sniffles, he looked into her eyes and said if that woman is mean to you, I'll send her away. Mollified April cuddled into his chest put her thumb into her mouth and fell asleep. He looked across at the other seat and said to Shawn, "What about it young man, think we can be a family someday?" "Sir, "said Shawn "do I need to go sort rocks today or would tomorrow be soon enough? I'm strong, I can find a lot." "No child, not today or tomorrow in fact no rock sorting ever." Shawn wrinkled his forehead, "Then what must I do to keep the little ones fed?" Shawn shook his head and spoke softly so that his voice didn't break. "Nothing Shawn. That's my job now. Your job is to get an education for now." Anne had fallen asleep about the same time as April, James in her arms. Shawn was yawning widely but struggling manfully to stay awake. He finally drifted off as they turned into the driveway. When the carriage stopped Sam sat for a minute bracing himself for the coming storm. Then he set the girls on the bench, checked to see everyone was asleep and exited the carriage. When he entered the house, he motioned the butler over. Find three people you can trust and bring them here. Tell cook to prepare tea and toast with lots of milk and perhaps a few scrambled eggs. I want my new family to have warm baths, a light dinner and then be tucked into bed. Put them in the West wing. When the servants arrived, he repeated his instructions and sent them to the carriage. Gearing up for battle he went in search of his mother. He found her on the patio at the back of the house with a tea tray. She looked furious. "Why are those people in my house?" Before she could get another word out, he rang for her maid and gave order that she was to pack enough for both of them for a few weeks away. He then sent for Brian and told him to guard the west wing door. He turned to his mother and explained that "those people" were her daughter

16

in law and grandchildren. As she started to sputter in anger he continued." You and your maid and the footman are going to Ohio. There is a small flat I had rented several months ago that you can stay in for now. Whether or not you may continue to live with servants and in modest comfort depends on you. Dad's will requested that I provide for you NOT that I allow you to ruin my life. You will have a small amount of spending money, but I will be paying the servants except for the footman. I hope he goes to jail. I hope they find charges that will keep him there for a long time. If you object or attempt to disrupt my life I know of several institutions that would be willing to have you live in them. Dad contributed to several and I intend to start that back up. Now if you have no questions, I think the carriage is waiting to take you to the next town over. I understand they have a small hotel there. Good night mother. Let me know if you are ready at some point to enjoy my family." With that Sam escorted her to the stable and helped her and her maid into the carriage. He saw that the footman was on the back and his trusted groom had the reins. The maid told him that she hadn't had time to pack much and Sam said he'd send the rest. Then he stopped and reached for the luggage. "I almost forgot the tradition of searching the luggage of anyone leaving town for good. Let me see what is in here." While his mother sputtered in protest Sam went through every bag. He confiscated his grandparent's jewelry when he found it as well as any of the antiques that were wrapped in his mother's dresses. The footman's things he dumped onto the ground, sifted through them and left them. He removed the uniforms stating that they belonged to his estate since the man was no longer employed by them. The man started to attack him at that point, but the groom grabbed him. Sam felt the pockets and lining and realized something was secreted there. The maid helped him when she learned that he now paid his salary not his mother and she told him everything she packed that shouldn't be there. It seems his mother had told her what to pack if they ever had to leave suddenly. With the luggage greatly reduced in weight the small party went on their way. When Sam tore apart the uniforms, he had confiscated he found a roll of bills that were probably part of a bribe, a small handgun, and several silver spoons and tiny objects d'art he though he remembered seeing in the dining room. He gathered the valuables up and went in search of his butler to ask him. The butler was pleased to see the pieces and told him of a couple maids that had been fired under suspicion of theft because they were gone. Sam handed him everything but the cash and gun and told him to make sure the doors were locked. Checking with the

18

maid who had been helping with the children he found that everyone was clean, fed and tucked into bed including his wife. He went to the library and sat down trying to get used to the fact that he was now a married man with four children and in charge of a mine that provided livelihood for many other families. First on his agenda was safety. Anne had lost her father and now her husband to shaft number four. He needed to see what could be done to prevent that from happening to anyone else. Reaching for paper and pen he began drafting letters and creating an agenda for a meeting with the miners the next morning. After several hours he went up the stairs satisfied that he had done all he could for now. As he passed the nursery, he peeked in. When he saw three beds and one crib empty, he went all the way into the room. He noticed that the door to the connecting room was open and peeked in there. Smiling he closed the door and went to his suite. After spending quite a bit of time on his knees discussing the situation with the Lord he vowed to stop worrying. Stretching out he was soon asleep.

Chapter 2

A New Beginning

Anne woke up a bit disoriented the next morning. She couldn't figure out why she was lying on such a comfortable surface. The last few days came back in a rush. Anne moaned and pressed her face into the pillow to hide the pain. Feeling something bump her she turned and discovered James waving his hands around as he greeted the day with his baby smiles. Knowing those smiles would soon turn to angry demands for food Anne snuck out of bed. That was quite difficult since Amy was draped across her legs and April was curled up on her other side. As she started to stand up, she realized Shawn was curled up in a blanket on the floor beside the bed. Holding James, she snuck into the nursery next door. On her way past the dresser she saw a note and grabbed it to read while James nursed. Last night she had been too tired to look around the nursery. Tucking the children in and praying with them was all she could manage. Wondering which of them had brought the baby into her as she changed James diaper, she surveyed the room. There were two sets of bunk beds and some tables with low chairs. A connecting door led to her bedroom and there was a private bathroom off the other side.   The beds all had warm fuzzy blankets and soft pillows. Settling into the rocking chair with James she opened the note. Anne, I hope you and the children slept well. I have some things to accomplish this morning but will be back to spend the afternoon with my family. It thrills me to write that. I know you don't feel like much of a family yet, but it will come. I see the children didn't enjoy their new accommodations. We will have to address that matter when I return. I am calling a meeting with the miners when shift change occurs today. By the time you read this it may be over. I am closing the mines for a time while safety policies are put in place to hopefully prevent further tragedy. I'll tell you all about it over lunch. Pull the rope when you and the little ones are ready for breakfast and someone will bring it. I hope you will share your preferences with the cook so you can all enjoy dining. Also, I took the liberty of having a representative from the store come to meet with you about clothes for you and the children.   They have some ready-made outfits that should suffice until the dressmaker arrives tomorrow. Anne dropped the note in shock, startling James who protested mightily at the interruption of his breakfast. Anne settled James back down crooning her apology. Shawn came in quietly and starred at the room. He came over to his mother and said, I guess I was too sleepy to really see this room last night. It's big isn't it. Anne smiled and said, "Go pull that rope over there and we'll see what kind of breakfast goes with a big room." She tucked the note into her pocket determined to have words about his plans to close the mine.   The others woke up and came crowding around her. Little ones talking about warm blankets and pillows while her two older ones just stared wide eyed at their new surroundings.   Hearing a knock on the door Anne called "Enter." The children stared amazed as three people carrying trays entered the room.   The maids set up a buffet on the high counter at the side of the room with dishes, silverware, napkins and bowls of food.   April spoke up, "I smell cooked stuff Mummy!" The third woman who entered smiled at that and said "I cooked stuff for you little one. I don't know what you and your brothers and sisters like, so I cooked a few different things." Turning to Anne she said, "Do you need anything special for the wee one? I made cream of wheat but wasn't sure if he was eating yet." Shawn inched a bit closer to the counter, turned and stared... "Mama they have eggs, lots of them." Not to be left out Amy chimed in. "Is it Christmas? there's jelly too." Embarrassed by the little ones carrying on she silenced all of them with a look and a nod. "Let's not have them thinking you weren't well fed." The maids finished and moved to the door. "I'm sure whatever you fix will be fine thank you" Anne said to the cook. Rising she placed James in the highchair and started to dish up plates for everyone. The children sat at the table eyes downcast. After they were alone, they all apologized for sounding poor. Amy piped up "Are we rich now Mummy?" Anne set the plates before them and replied, "Well I don't really know, but I do know we are grateful and can remember manners." Shawn rose and held his mother's chair. April clasped her hands and started grace. Even James stilled as her little voice sang "Thank you Lord for this food and for the roof over our head." Then she looked up and said "Mummy I can't thank Him for us all together cause Daddy's gone" Anne thought for a minute and suggested "how about we thank Him that we are all safe.? Now let's have some of this wonderful food." The children quickly devoured the eggs and oatmeal. James managed to taste a biscuit crumb or two while he crumbled the tiny piece he'd been given. Anne ate because she had to fuel her body to take care of everyone and because she needed strength to discuss the mine with Sam. After everyone was done Shawn organized clean up. Everyone carrying something they went out the door and down the stairs in search of the kitchen. When they found it, they marched up to the cook and said

Thank you for the wonderful breakfast, went to the sink and started dishes. The young lad seated at the table looked shocked but then ran up and took the towels out of the children's hands. "Wait that's my job" he yelled. "My Mom needs the money I earn here doing dishes every day." In panic he looked from Anne to the cook. "Children," Anne called "We mustn't take this boys job away, we'll have other chores than the ones we had at" Anne started to say home but quickly turned it into "The other house." The man she vaguely remembered guarding the door of the wing they were shown last night came into the room. "The representative from the store is here to see you now Ma'am. If you would come this way?" Nodding to the cook she patted the boy's shoulder, whispered "Sorry" and followed. They all went up to the nursery where a young woman was unpacking a box of toys. There seemed to be something for each of the children as well as crayons and white paper and blocks. Amy and April were each handed Raggedy Anne dolls and Shawn received a toy boat. James happily chewed on a small ring toy. The young woman said "Mr. King told us to just bring one small thing each but you can pick what else you think you might need from this catalog. He wasn't sure of sizes, but he wanted me to bring 2 outfits for each of you and 2 pair of shoes. If you could tell me sizes, I can show you what I have." Shawn stopped playing with his plane and stared at her. "3 outfits? Why do we need more than 1?" Anne tilted her head at him and raised an eyebrow. He said, "I'm sorry I didn't mean to be disrespectful; I was just wondering." "I would imagine that we need a church outfit, one to wear and one to wash." said Anne as she reached into the box and helped the girl who said her name was Leah, to find the right sizes. By the time they had 3 each everyone was exhausted. James slept with his new toy still clutched in his pudgy fist. The others were curled up in the beds. The girls seemed to be introducing their new dolls to their ragged dolls Anne had made the year before out of an old apron and some yarn pieces. Shawn was looking at a book he had found in the corner bookcase while holding his boat in one hand. Leah smiled. "Let me know if you need anything else" My Dad and I run the store one town over. Anne gathered her three new dresses and went next door to change. Carefully hanging the others up, she examined her old dress to see if the fabric was good enough to make into doll clothes or a small bag for Shawn to carry books in. When she heard a slight knock on the door to the hall, she hurried to open it. Sam was standing there smiling. "You look beautiful this morning although I admit you were even more beautiful surrounded by our little ones this morning when I left the note." At

Anne's sharp intake of breath, he added "I had a
maid check to see if everyone was decent before I
popped in." Frowning she whispered fiercely "what
do you mean by the atrocities you wrote about in
this missive?" Motioning him in she pushed the door
to the nursery closed a bit. She noticed he had left
the hallway door open and that pleased her. Pointing
him to a chair on the opposite side of the room she
sat across from him and demanded "Why would you
shut down the mine, that is our livelihood well not
ours, I don't know what ours is but everyone down
in town depends on that mine for everything. How
could you put all those people out of work just like
that? I know it's dangerous but so is starvation which
is what you just sent 90% of the town into." "Wait
Anne," let me explain Sam protested. "They won't
starve, there are other jobs, and this is just
temporary." "Anything more temporary than a
couple hours will cost some of them their lives.
Don't you understand? We don't have reserves of
cash or a stocked pantry. We have food for a day if
we're lucky and cutlery for two people. We take
turns eating because the company only allows 2
dishes or utensils and one pan. None of us have the
money to buy more and those that save and get
another know that when the crates are searched
before they leave, they'll be confiscated even if we
show a bill of sale." Anne finished in a rush and

Sam reached out and grabbed her hands. "Please Anne listen, I plan to solve all that, but safety has to come first. Men are coming to inspect the mines and tell us what we must do to make them safe. In the meantime, the men will work on other jobs. No one will lose any pay, I promise. I am going to look at production and costs and hope to raise their pay in fact. Trust me it will get better in the town.   Some of the men will be fixing the houses. I have the foreman going house to house now to see what is needed to get them up to a good standard. Some houses need to be torn down but first I have a group of men building another section with more space in between the houses. It's a fire trap down there now. Some will be cutting timber to shore up the tunnels. Others are building a schoolhouse and a church. There is plenty of work available. I'm also implementing bonuses for the number of years worked. The men grumbled a bit but seemed willing to try it. The women that were there want the houses fixed so I think it will work out. I'll reopen the mines as soon as it is safe. I'm hoping you can tell me who would be best to talk to about how they are treated by the foremen. I also want to find out about the company store. I had the general store in Roberts deliver because I've never liked how the manager here treats people. For now, let's feed these hungry little ones" pointing at the connecting door. Anne glanced over and saw little fingers holding the door shut and heard Shawn's voice shushing April. She rose and asked "anyone hungry again? Three children rushed in while the fourth yelled in protest at being left alone. Sam scooped up the girls and said, "let's go see what's for lunch!" Anne hurried to pick up James and with a hand on Shawn's shoulder followed down the stairs. Instead of turning into the kitchen he went for the next door which opened onto a dining hall. The children climbed up onto the chairs but could hardly see the table. "Fiona," Sam called "we need some risers for these chairs please." A few minutes later she hurried in with several large books. Anne helped each one climb up and then helped Brian settle James in his chair. When they were all ready the dishes were uncovered to reveal heaping plates of ham, sweet potatoes and corn on the cob. Sam laughed, "this was my favorite meal when I was your age Shawn. What's your favorite?" "I like bread and butter." he answered "but this looks great." The lunch was loud boisterous and messy and when it was over three little ones were drooping over empty plates. James was already asleep. He'd gone down while Anne was cleaning up his hands and face. Smiling Sam nodded to Brian and Fiona who each picked up a sleepy girl. Sam scooped up Shawn despite his protests that he could walk and led the way upstairs. Tucking the little ones in was the most fun he'd ever had. Tiptoeing out he asked Anne to come to the library. Fiona took a seat in the nursery and pulled out some mending. "I'll call if they wake Ma'am," she reassured Anne. Entering the library Sam invited Anne to sit in one of the chairs facing the fireplace. Silent for a minute he just looked at her. "You are beautiful, and I am so grateful that you've agreed to give me a family. I have tons of questions for you about living in town and the company store but let's cover the important things first. Have the children been to school yet? They all seem bright but I'm afraid to ask what the school is like down there." Anne shocked him by replying "Donald always used your gifts to afford school. I have the money he'd put aside. Since the footman didn't search us, I have everything we were able to save. I was hoping we could continue that until the money is gone. I think there's enough for each of the little ones to finish 6th grade." Raising his hand Sam stared at her "Afford, it costs you to send the children to school?" Now it was Anne's turn to be shocked. "Well, yes isn't it supposed to? Besides school costs, we lose the child's income when they are at school all day." The public-school system in Pennsylvania started in 1834. It should be provided by the state. Shaking his head, Sam rose and went to the desk where he removed a folder and a pad of paper. Sitting back down he said,

"Schooling is supposed to be free. I don't know if the teacher is skimming or it was my mother's idea but from now on it is free and I'm getting another teacher as well. If this one was dishonest enough to take fees when his salary was coming in then I don't want him teaching the children of this town. I wonder how good a teacher he had been. I will require everyone to send their children and before you tell me they need the kid's income; I am raising salaries to cover that problem. I want the kids to be in school until they are at least 16 from now on." Anne shook her head, "They start in the mines at 14 remember and at 10 they can work above ground picking up coal and separating rocks." At Sam's confused look she explained that the mine dumps debris in a large pile. The children from 10 to 14 can climb around in it looking for pieces of coal that were missed. They hardly ever found much, sometimes enough to get a few pennies. Most of the time they filled their pockets with coal dust for the stove at home. "Children that age should be running around, climbing trees, fishing and learning not earning their bread. Please Anne help me make this better?" Handing her the tablet he said "I want you to write down everything you remember from life in town, all the hidden costs, what the company owns, everything. We can discuss each point over the next few weeks." For now, though I want to talk about our family. I want you to interview governesses," seeing her stiffen he added " I know you'll be raising our children, but I need you to help me as well. Perhaps the governess could supervise some of their activities from time to time, so you have the time for other things. I heard from Hunter that the children tried to take over his job this morning. He needed a bit of reassurance that the other chores we find them won't interfere with his supporting his mother. I thought perhaps we could come up with something they can do to learn responsibility other than dishes?" Anne admitted she had been trying to come up with something that wouldn't interfere with anyone's job but was open to his suggestions. "Good, let's take a walk and I'll show you what I was thinking. Fiona will tell us if they need you. Leading her outside he pointed to the garden. I thought perhaps they could help Gerald with the garden. He has a flower garden that he guards fiercely but perhaps the vegetable garden could be shared? I'm sure he'd enjoy help with the weeding, watering and picking. He won't feel his job is in jeopardy because I'm adding to his duties. He'll be a teacher and supervisor for the children. He has children of his own and is very good with them I assure you." "Gardening" smiled Anne "that would be wonderful. We'll have to come up with something for winter, and I want them to make their own beds as well though." "When do you think they'll be sleeping in them?" asked Sam. "I wanted to address that problem also." Concerned, Anne stopped and faced him. "They just lost their father, their house and everything normal to them, surely you don't begrudge them some comfort?" "I want them comfortable, but I also want you comfortable and I don't think you'll get proper sleep sharing that bed with 3 others besides someday I hope you share with one other." Anne bit her lip and looked down. Sam hurried to add. "I planned to move another bed into the nursery for you to sleep on for now. When they are content there you can transition into the other room." "That may work" said Anne "but where does the governess sleep?" "There is another room off the nursery set up for the governess. Let's visit the stable with the children this afternoon. I have a few ideas for chores there as well." Anne nodded thoughtfully. When they returned to the house, they found happy chaos in the nursery. Snacks had arrived in the form of hot bread and apple butter. Fiona was on the floor playing with April while James sat happily in her lap gnawing on a crust. Shawn and Amy were still at the table finishing up a snack. Fiona looked up when they came in and started to scramble to her feet. "Oh Ma'am, Sir, I was just" Anne stopped her "you were just taking excellent care of my children. Stay. they are happy." Shawn came running over to Sam.

"Can we explore Sir? We're all rested and not
hungry except for James maybe." Sam stooped to his
level and said "We'll have to find something for you
to call me, won't we? Yes, we can explore. Let's
look around outside since the weather is
cooperating. We'll save the house explorations for a
rainy day. Glancing up at Anne he asked, how long
until you and James are ready to join us? We'll start
in the garden and meet you there." Ushering the
little ones out he glanced at Fiona. "Good job by the
way, perhaps you should consider applying for the
governess job?" Fiona smiled and bobbed a curtsy,
"Thank you Sir, I'd love that." Just then April
knocked over her milk glass. Seeing that Sam
laughed, "Are you sure?" Fiona just nodded and
helped her clean it up. When things were cleaned up,
he herded the three oldest out the door and down the
stairs. The children happily ran ahead of him glad to
be outside. When they got to the garden fence, they
came to a full stop for standing his arms crossed was
Gerald. He looked at them and demanded they form
a line in age order. Then he glanced up at Sam and
said, "you can be last." Cautioning them to stay in
line so they didn't disturb any of the tiny sprouts he
led them thru the plot pointing out different areas.
When they were back to the gate, he handed them
mats and had them sit cross legged on them.
Explaining that they should avoid sitting on the wet

ground he asked what plants the children liked best. Shawn spoke up first "I don't know what some of the things are that you said were growing in there." Startled Gerald crouched down. "Well then let's do this a bit differently. I'll list what we are growing, and you stop me when I need to explain. OK? Green beans, yellow beans." April laughed and said, "beans don't come in colors like flowers, they're just green." "Well, this garden has yellow and green beans." said Gerald. "Now how about corn, carrots, and squash? "What's a squash" asked Amy shyly. "Well a squash can be many different things. Have you ever seen a pumpkin? or zucchini?" Shawn shook his head "no Sir, never." While his eyes widened Gerald was careful to not show surprise. He described zucchini, watermelon, cucumbers, lettuce, potatoes, turnips and many other plants. The children were enthralled. "Now it is time to pick what plants you want to be responsible for." said Sam. "Your Mother and I decided that your chore for now would be to help in the vegetable garden. You will each pick a type of plant and it will be yours to take care of." April smiled, "Can we take it upstairs to watch it grow?" Hearing a soft giggle behind him Sam turned to see Anne holding a happy James. "Does James have to work too?" asked Amy "I think he might be a bit too small yet to help in the garden." smiled Sam. "Perhaps his chore can be keeping us smiling. What would each of you like to plant?" April spoke up first. "I want beans. I want to see the new colored ones." Amy quickly followed with "I want to grow those big orange squishy things you told us about." Shawn looked thoughtful. "I think I'd like to grow something red. What did you say was red?" "That could be the tomatoes or maybe radishes. Did you want the ones that grow under the ground or above it? replied Gerald. "Can I do both please I'm older and can work faster than the girls can." "Certainly, but you must all promise to never come to the garden without an adult. I have two helpers, Albert and Bruce. They can work with you too. I wish you could have been here to plant the seeds but perhaps we can plant a different kind of seed in the greenhouse and those you can take inside little miss, if your parents agree. We can get started in the morning then. Now off with you there is more to explore!" The children jumped up and started away. "Wait" Gerald yelled, "the mats. I'm not cleaning up after you. You must learn to put things away!" " We know sir, sorry we just got excited. Are you sure it's not Hunter's job" said Amy, "he's supporting his mother." Looking confused Gerald showed the children how to hang the mats to dry and away they went.   As they crossed the grass Sam chased first one then the other until they all arrived squealing at the stables. "Looky looky" squealed April, "big dogs." Shawn frowned, "those aren't dogs silly they are um small cows?" A voice from inside the fence said "Goats, my boy they are goats. We don't have cows here." vaulting over the gate Adam faced the children. "Are these my new workers Mr. Sam" he asked? "I thought there were four of them." April peeked from behind her mother's skirts where she had run when she heard the word dog. Smiling Adam held out his hand to her. "Would you like to be the first to see my new baby goat he offered." "There's no dogs?" she asked. "Well there is but she wouldn't hurt a pretty little thing like you. She loves little girls and boys." Now Amy stepped back "loves, like to eat?" "No no no" Adam burst out she loves to play with them not eat them in fact once she figures out you live here; she will protect you with her life." "Really like from the town dogs." asked Shawn? Sam cocked an eyebrow at Anne. "Put that on the list will you dear?" Anne smiled, "Already on it." Adam repeated "She will protect you from anything. But let's meet the newest goat." Opening the gate, he encouraged the children to come see. In the corner a tiny goat lay with her mother on a pile of hay. The other goats came up to see the newcomers to their pasture and the children stayed very close to Anne. Putting a hand on April's head he said "don't be afraid I'm calling the dog in." Adam let out a shrill whistle and through a low barn window hurtled a black and white dog. Ulric raised his hand and pointed to the far corner. She rounded up the 3 goats and sent them running that way before April had a chance to scream. "Now that Bella has the goats where they won't bother us let's take a look at that baby." April crouched down. "She's littler than James!" Rising unsteadily the little one curiously approached. "Quiet now so you don't scare her" cautioned Ulric. Holding her breath Amy slowly put out a hand and could hardly keep from screaming when the tiny black nose touched her fingers. both the child and the goat immediately ran to their mothers, bravery given up for the time. "Would you like to name her? All our goats have names, but no one has named her yet. She was only born a couple hours ago." "Wow, James was born six months ago, and he can't even stand yet" said April. "Well" said Sam "People aren't always as advanced as animals are." Nodding wisely Shawn agreed with him and then asked, "do you have any other animals?" The adults turned immediately to the gate avoiding each other's eyes. Under his breath Sam whispered, "This is the best, absolute best." Adam and Anne started coughing. The children looked up confused and Anne said "dust must have gotten in our throats but we're fine. What shall we name the baby? "Is it a boy goat or a girl goat?" asked Amy. Adam said. "It's a little girl. That's

called a Nanny goat. Boys are called Billie goats."
"Then let's call it Lady." Said Amy. The other
children nodded. "Lady it is.' Said Sam. "What are
the names of the other goats?" asked April. "The
other three are named Daisy, Violet and Lupine."
Replied Adam as he pointed them out. "Gerald's
oldest daughter named them. She's about your age
Shawn." Shawn frowned at that, "Yeah but she's a
girl." He commented. "Now, can we see the other
animals?" At the door of the stable Adam stopped
and made each child promise to never enter without
an adult. Horses are big and don't always see
children in the way when they are moving around so
no visits without a grownup he insisted. Moving in
they could see five heads looking curiously over
their stable doors. April found her mother's skirts
again. Leading the way Adam introduced each of
them. "This beauty is Candy. She and Apple pulled
the carriage when you arrived yesterday. These two
handsome gentlemen are King and Jack. They are
stronger and usually pull the wagon. Can anyone tell
me the differences you see?" April pulled her thumb
out of her mouth "Bigger" she whispered. "Yes, the
boys are bigger anything else?" Amy studied them
carefully. "Those have more hair on their necks."
"Yes, this type of horse has a thicker mane." Shawn
commented that they were a different color. "These
boys are called Percherons they love to work hard.

These girls are hard workers too but usually don't have to pull as heavy a load. They are Belgians." explained Adam. "Who's that?" asked Shawn pointing at another horse. Looking up at Sam he continued, "You rode him yesterday, is he yours? "He's mine" said Sam. "His name is Sugar because of his coloring. He's an Arabian. "Who wants to pet them?" Shawn was the only one brave enough until Sam offered to pick up the girls so they could see better. When he did that, they were brave enough to pet each nose that was thrust at them. James was chortling happily as Anne rubbed Apple's nose. Sam set the girls on a nearby bench and grabbed a carrot from a nearby bin. The four horse immediately leaned their noses as close to him as they could, and the children watched him break it into five pieces and feed one to each. Adam smiled, "I remember teaching you how to do that Mr. Sam. I've been hoping to teach your children to do the same someday." April pulled on his pantleg. He looked down and found her pointing to another stall. "Wondering about that noise are you little one? Well let's go see, shall we?" Taking her hand, he led her to the stall where he picked her up so she could peer over the edge. Shawn let out a delighted "Puppies, Mama they have puppies" when he looked, and Amy immediately went to Sam to be picked up so she could see. Adam whistled again and Bella came thru the small entrance in the back of the stall. April's grip tightened on Ulric's neck as did Amy on Sam's, but Shawn wasn't afraid. "Can I please go in please?" "Well that's up to Bella" said Sam. "She will decide if you can be trusted with her little ones or not. If she pushes you away you must obey her. Ready to try?" Sam opened the door and entered the stall; Shawn close beside him. He sat on a bale of hay, Shawn mimicking his every move. Calling Bella to him he rubbed her ears and crooned lovely things to her. Then he took Shawn's hand in his and offered it to Bella. The dog took her time sniffing him all over and after a few minutes licked his face. Shawn laughed and petted her telling her how wonderful she was. Sam looked up at Anne and patted the hay bale next to him. Without hesitation Anne seated herself still holding James and they were treated to the same sniff test and shortly accepted even though James poked her a couple times. Anne stopped him and apologized but Bella seemed to understand he was a baby. Amy came hesitantly over to Sam and sat on his knee. Bella waited politely until Sam invited her over to sniff and lick yet another new person. Last of all April slowly came forward. Bella immediately lay down and rolled over in front of her and April giggled. At that sound Bella jumped up and began licking her until April was seated in the straw shrieking with delight. A whimper in the corner made Bella turn and jump the low board that kept her pups contained. The children crawled over and sat watching as she nuzzled three little ones. Behind her Sam and Anne held a whispered conference. Anne frowned but finally nodded. Sam whispered something in Adam's ear, and he started climbing the ladder to the loft with a large box in his hands. Sam called Shawn. Shawn reluctantly left the puppies and came over. "Yes Sir?" he said looking over his shoulder at the corner. "Still need to fix that name." muttered Sam. "Shawn do you feel you could learn to train a dog to be as useful as Bella?" "I'd like to try." he answered "but I know dogs cost a whole lot, but can I come see them sometimes? I'll only come in with an adult like I promised." "Shawn, dogs do cost a lot but mainly a lot of time. You see Bella needs a helper since her job just got bigger. I was thinking of keeping one of her puppies, but I don't think I will have time to train it. Adam is pretty busy too so maybe you could do it?" suggested Sam.   Shawn straightened up, "yes sir that is I can try sir will you really let me have a dog Mama? You always said no before." "Well, now I'm saying yes but you must take care of it. I don't want chewed shoes or messes around." "You mean I can keep it in the house? WOW which one can I have?" asked Shawn excitedly. Adam was back with a big box that he set outside the stall. He explained that the pups couldn't leave their mother for another few days or so, but Shawn could come every day and watch them so when the time came, he would know which one was to be his. "That gives you time to come up with a good name as well." said Anne. The girls walked over looking sad. "When will we be old enough to have dogs?" asked Amy? "Well," said Sam "I think one dog in the house and one outside is enough for us but" and then he pointed the two sad little girls to the doorway where Adam now stood holding the box again. "Let's go see what he has." suggested Anne. The girls scrambled out and the adults followed smiling at each other. Carefully closing the stall door Adam invited the girls to sit on the hay bale. Then he opened the box in front of them. "Kittens" squealed April. "Mama they have kittens.   Can we have one please?" Sam reached into the box and picked up a beautiful grey kitten and placed it in Amy's lap. Then he took the white one and handed it to April.   The girls bent over the babies murmuring like they used to when they were allowed to hold James as a newborn. After a bit Anne asked," What are you going to name them?" and the girls looked up startled. "You mean she's mine" they said at the same time? Sam nodded but admonished "you must take care of them or they come back to the barn." "We will" the girls chorused. Shawn came to the door to see them and looked a bit sad. "Wish my pup was old enough to come with me but I understand sir." Sam frowned at the sir but nodded. "Good job" he said. "Now let's go get cleaned up for dinner, shall we?" The girls jumped up with kittens in their arms, can we bring them "please please please?" Ulric nodded, "They are old enough now to leave their Mom. I'll be looking for homes for the others shortly anyway. "Anne looked up and said, "Wait on that Adam I may have a couple ideas." On the way to the house she whispered her idea to Sam who gave a delighted laugh. "I knew you'd be a great partner! Let's get started tomorrow. Did you and Fiona reach an agreement today?" "Yes, in fact she should have moved her stuff into the nursery by now." replied Anne. "The nursery?" questioned Sam? "Yes, and her brother will be arriving tomorrow to take the governess room. He just graduated from Normal school and can teach the children until you need him in town to be the teacher." "Awesome!" shouted Sam delightedly, "two more things off my list. You're amazing!" April ran back to them and said, "You're slow! come on" and they all ran to the house. Fiona was waiting for them in the nursery and dinner for the children was laid out on the table. The children eagerly ran to wash their hands all trying to tell Fiona about the garden and stables at once.

Chapter 3

Planning

Anne and Sam walked down to the library. When they sat down Anne pulled a piece of paper out of her pocket. Sam grabbed a tablet and prepared to take notes. "Tell me about the dogs." Said Sam. Anne frowned. "I don't know how to solve the feral dog problem without shooting them, but we need to fix that right away. They have been known to attack children on their way to school and woman never walk alone. Everyone carries a stick when we go to different sections. Last year they killed a woman and her baby as she was picking berries. We never found the babies body and the woman had been torn up. " Shuddering Sam asked, "Did someone tell my mother this was going on?" "Yes, she suggested we use poison or shoot them. None of us could afford it although Don did put some out around our place at one point after I had the baby. You provided the money for that when you sent a gift. You do know that wasn't why we told you of the children, don't you?" Nodding thoughtfully Sam made a note on his tablet. "Perhaps traps would be helpful. If I loan them out, they shouldn't be too prideful to take them.

I'll tell them I want the problem cleared up so the miners can focus on their work more and worry about their family less. What do you think?" Anne smiled and said, "I'm so glad you understand about the men's pride. It is hard to help them. Charity will not work. They won't take it, but they will take a loan of equipment to help their family especially if they feel you are asking to help yourself." "Good, because I plan to use the same tactic when I give out the kittens. Mice bring disease and that cuts down on productivity. I want those men able to work. I don't want the cats turning feral though so I hope the children will tame them. I'll appoint an inspector to make sure the problem is clearing up and that the cats are taken care of. Perhaps one of the miner's wives could take on the task? Or one of the retired miners.? " queried Sam. "We don't have retired miners Sam, if someone wants to leave or can't work anymore, they aren't welcome in town. Sometimes another family will take them in but there are no retirement benefits if that's what you're thinking. None of us can save for that." Sam shook his head "I've got a lot to make up for, don't I? I could become a pauper and it still wouldn't be enough." After a solemn moment Anne said, "Let's not think of it as making up, let's think of it as moving forward. You don't have to atone for your Mother's mistakes, you must make the mines a profitable place where people can work to support their family. Which brings me to a question." Anne hesitated and looked at him. He smiled encouragingly but was silent. "What do we have to live on? I mean I see goats, horses, three gardeners, at least two maids, a cook, butler, now a governess and a teacher. The footman seems to have disappeared and I have no idea what else. Oh except for the dishwasher, I remember him. If you want me to run your house, I need to know how many people I have charge of and what they are paid. Did I overstep in hiring Fiona's brother? Can we afford to pay the men more and implement the changes you are suggesting?" "I'm glad you asked Anne." replied her husband. "I want you to understand the books as well as I do. The mine produces a great deal of coal and coal sells well right now. I hope to open another couple shafts in case any of the four we now have been played out. We have savings, lots of savings which I mean to use half of to implement the changes. The men will be paid according to what they produce. Well, let me clarify that a bit. They will have a reasonable salary with a bonus based on what they produce. We'll still own the homes, but they will be sturdy and as safe as we can make them. If they want to buy them, I'm willing to sell them. The prices in the store will be set to provide a reasonable profit for the storekeeper but nothing for us. We'll keep an eye on it though, so the prices don't get out of line. Credit will be available as it is now, but interest will be reduced. I have the books here to see what is owed and will make sure the men weren't being gouged which I think they were. If I were to adjust the totals, would the men notice do you think? I can use the excuse that I found the interest being charged was exorbitant. I don't feel wiping the debt would be good for the men, but I hate that almost everyone owes more than they make. I would like to work out reasonable payments and give a discount for cash. Do you think they would accept that? "

"Yes, if you word it carefully and respect them. I think they would and if they don't their wives will make them." But we got sidetracked a bit there. While I do want to hear about your plans for town, I need to start running this household and I need information." Sam reminded her that he had only come into the household after years away and really didn't have all the information she wanted. "I can tell you what we can afford to pay in salaries and how much I plan to give you each month to pay for food and clothing. Other than that, I really don't know. You need to talk to Brian. He has been running the household for years. He'll tell you all you need to know. I doubt he'll have trouble relinquishing the reins, he's been with us for years and is very reasonable. Set up a meeting with him and let me know if you need anything else. Oh, I'd like to start giving Shawn some pocket money if you don't object. I feel he needs to learn how to use money from a young age. He would be responsible for giving some to the church, saving some and having a bit of spending money. He can save for toys or a new bridle for his pony, whatever he wants." Anne nodded, "That sounds fine, wait what? did you say pony? What are you talking about? There's no pony out there. Those horses are too big for him to ride or brush or whatever you have planned. You were trying to slip that in while I was distracted, weren't you?" Sam laughed, "Not really but I wondered what you'd say if I brought it up. I know he's too little for the horses I have but the kids need a pony. It will teach them responsibility and help them learn to be comfortable around horses and to ride. I had one growing up and I've always planned on making sure my children did as well. I'll get a gentle one who is used to children and it would belong to all of them not just Shawn. I really think it is important and I'm not trying to spoil them I promise. I'd love to but I understand why I shouldn't." "All right you can get him a pony, but I want to learn to ride as well. That way I can be with them when they are off exploring." Their talk turned to other things like favorite foods and what they liked to read. After another hour, Brian knocked lightly on the door and announced, "Dinner is served." Rising Sam offered his arm to Anne and they moved to the dining room. It was the first time she had seen the room in its formal state. The dinner china was beautiful, and the crystal shined. A maid stood by the door at attention and Brian stood at the other end of the room also at attention. Sam held Anne's chair and seated himself. Immediately Brian brought wine and presented it to Sam who nodded. He then poured it into the glass closest to their plate. He also provided water in one of the glasses. The maid came around with a platter on which were small bowls of salad. When they had finished that course, she came back and cleared all the plates and set others down. The platter she held out had a beautiful cut of beef sliced very thin surrounded by small roasted potatoes. On the table were bowls of green beans, beets and baskets of rolls. There were other courses, but Anne was too overwhelmed to remember what they were. She looked at Sam who was heartily eating. "Are we expecting to eat this way every night? This is way too much food for two people. Are the children eating this much?" Sam caught her hand, "I know this is different for you and you can make changes if you want but the extra food goes to the staff I think, no, the children don't eat this much or this richly and yes, most people in our station do eat this way every night." Anne looked troubled. "If the children don't eat this way why would you think it healthy for us? or for the staff? I can see when we are entertaining or at holidays, but I feel we need to make some changes.   The poor cook is overworked if she has to do this every night or are there helpers I haven't met yet?" Sam put down his fork and stared at her. "I've never thought about it much. You may be right about the rich food, my father died of a heart attack at a pretty young age and he was quite overweight. Perhaps we need to implement some changes here as well. That is up to you since you'll be planning menus with Cook. Should I assume that you have no interest in the chocolate cake cook spent all afternoon icing because it is my favorite? Or the sherry that Brian is ready to pour to go with it?" Anne turned and saw the maid holding aloft a large chocolate 3-tiered cake with thick frosting swirls. "Oh my, well I guess we've gone this far with the meal we should finish it although I don't want the sherry really." After slices of cake were reduced to crumbs Anne and Sam went back to the library but not before Anne told Brian that she would like to meet with him as soon as possible. Anne hastened to assure him that he should eat dinner first, including a piece of that cake before coming. When they entered the library, Anne spent some time perusing the shelves enjoying the thought that here was reading material for years. On a low shelf she found children's books. Sam watched her from the desk. "My father felt everyone in the house should enjoy the library, so he had some of my books put on a shelf. He wanted me to feel coming to the library and reading were not reserved for adulthood. He never disciplined me in here as some of my classmates told me their fathers did. They were afraid to come to the library because it meant they were in trouble. Instead I spent many wonderful hours curled up in a chair while he worked or sitting on his lap while he read to me. When I needed discipline, he came to me and we went for a walk. He came to the nursery or schoolroom other times as well and we took plenty of walks not related to my misbehavior also. I want to do the same with our children. I don't ever want them to dread seeing me or hearing my tread on the porch. He approved of my friendship with Donald." They fell silent after that each in their own thoughts. It was not an uncomfortable silence though. Shortly after that Brian knocked and entered the study. Sam invited him to sit down and handed Anne a pad and pencil. Anne looked up and repeated the invitation to be seated. When he didn't move, she added, "I'd like to be able to look at you without getting a crick in my neck please?" Nodding he perched on the edge of one of the chairs. "Thank you, I won't keep you long, but I need your help. As the wife of the head of the house I need to know who works here and what each of their jobs are. I would guess that I need to meet with cook and perhaps a few others as well so I can get a handle on who does what around here. I'm not trying to replace you nor insinuate that you aren't doing an excellent job just trying to make sure I know who is around my family and what they do. I understand that salaries have not been the best in the past and that many people have left due to my mother in laws requirements.   I'd like us to work together to make things fair for everyone here. Can you give me a list of people we employ, their salaries and their duties? I'd also like you to arrange for me to meet with each one individually so I can talk with them." Brian smiled politely" Of course Ma'am I would be glad to help with that. Would tomorrow afternoon be soon enough? I can have it ready for you around ten tomorrow. Let me know when you want to start meeting with the staff. Perhaps tomorrow afternoon? Did you want to meet with the outside staff as well or will that continue under the master's domain?" I want to meet with them because they will be watching my children when they are doing chores and helping them learn." replied Anne. " I'm sure my husband will continue to oversee their duties, however. Brian, I hope you don't see this as my taking over. I will be very busy helping Sam revamp the town, teaching the woman how to cope with the changes, and raising my children so I expect to leave most of the day to day running of the house to you. I want to make sure you have enough funds to adequately pay salaries, any bonuses, and the bills. I would like to do Christmas myself but will take advice if that's ok with you?" "Christmas Ma'am?" Brian looked confused. " I don't know what you mean so I'm glad you'll take that on. We decorate a bit downstairs but I'm not sure what else you would want. Anne interrupted him at that point. "Do you mean there are no decorations in here or other rooms of the house? Were there no presents for the staff?" Brian was startled. "We haven't been allowed to decorate since Mr. Sam's father died. We were told it was a waste of money. Our present was being able to keep our job another year. I'll continue to perform in whatever capacity you require, and I might add I am glad you are here. The children are wonderful and really give this place some new life. We all love having them. I should also tell you that one of the maids has given notice. She is getting married to someone out west somewhere. I believe she is a mail order bride for a farmer. Unless you want her to leave earlier, she will be gone next week.?" Anne smiled, "How nice for her. What is usually done when a member of the staff leaves or gets married?" "Done Ma'am?" Brian looked confused. "Sometimes the notice is refused and he or she is required to leave before they had planned. Otherwise they take their one crate which the footman always searches and walk to the next town over. " Anne and Sam both frowned at that and Sam said. "That is not acceptable. Please see that when she leaves, she has a ride to the train station and have her come see one of us for a small gift for her. As to the crate. I will leave it up to you if it needs to be searched or not. You know the staff better than we do. Have Gerald give you some seeds for her as well, both flower and vegetable ones so she can have a bit of home to comfort her out there." Brian looked a bit stunned as he left the room. Anne and Sam spent the rest of the evening talking about what they would need to discuss with the miners next week and came up with a partial agenda for the meeting.

Safety

Houses

Store

School

Animals

By the time they had that much done they were both exhausted and having trouble keeping their eyes open. They walked up the stairs side by side and at her door. Sam kissed her hand and wished her pleasant dreams. Continuing to his room he thought back over the day and how much he was enjoying having a family. After getting ready for bed he went to the Lord asking for help in making them all feel at home and that he be able to raise them to be the kind of adults that would follow Him. He snuck in a prayer that someday Anne would accept him as her husband in every way before saying Amen and climbing into bed. Meanwhile Anne was also on her knees praying for her children as well. She also prayed for their future spouses and asked that she be able to love Sam someday. Wearily she fell into bed luxuriating in the space but knowing it would be temporary. The children still didn't spend the night in their own beds.

The next morning Sandy showed up with bolts of
fabric and boxes of patterns. The children groaned
when Anne insisted, they stand still and be measured
before getting to go outside to see Gerald or Adam.
After being tortured with this for an hour they
happily ran outside. Shawn hurrying to the pups.
"Name him today." called Anne after him. The
kittens whose named were Snow and Storm, thought
the fabric bolts were a new type of scratching post
so they were banished from the room quickly. Anne
made short work of choosing serviceable fabrics and
patterns that would allow the children to move
freely. She also chose fabric for matching dresses
for the girls for formal wear and suits for the boys.
There were several bolts of soft fabric for pajamas
and one that would be perfect for diapers. She
showed Sandy to a room where there were shelves
to hold the bolts and a table for cutting. Sandy
promised to have everything ready as soon as
possible but seemed daunted by the task set before
her. She looked at Anne said Ma'am I don't have a
helper, and this is a big order. Smiling Anne
suggested she hire one of the women who was
known for her ability to use a needle. She offered to
send for her so Sandy could evaluate her abilities
and hire her on a temporary basis and she happily

agreed. Anne went in search of Brian to see if anyone was available to run the errand. Howard was dispatched with the message to come and to bring her son as well. Anne then went in search of the children and found Gerald frowning at her eldest while holding onto the pup. Keeping out of sight she learned that the pup had not been closely watched while the children were playing and had dug up part of the garden. Gerald told Shawn that the dog was not welcome past the gate and must be taught this. "What do you think we should do about the mess he made? " "Shawn frowned, "I don't know Mr. Gerald. I would fix it if I knew how."   Gerald looked down at the boy and said, "Well I don't have time to undo his work. I think you need to learn how to replant that area or we'll not have enough peas for the table this year. They'll be late as it is." "Yes sir, but I don't like peas and neither do my sisters so maybe we don't need as many as you might think. " Gerald suddenly had to cough for a bit before he replied and Fiona, who had joined Anne in her hiding place, clapped a hand over her mouth. Anne's eyes were watering but she managed a solemn face. She walked the rest of the way to Shawn and put a hand on his shoulder. "What happened here?" she asked innocently. "Titan dug up the peas." glumly answered her son. "Well, I'm glad he has a name, but we must fix this, I love peas." Shawn looked up at Gerald. "May I come out during my free time this afternoon and fix the peas?" Gerald nodded, "I'll assign Albert to show you how." Now go find Adam and start training that pup of yours." Anne thanked him for dealing so kindly with the child and he smiled at her. "Your children are a joy. I have a couple near that age. Perhaps I could bring them by to play sometime?" Yes of course that would be wonderful." Leaving Fiona who was teaching the girls how to make a daisy chain she went to the porch to wait for Howard to return. Pulling the pad and pencil from her pocket she began to make another list. When the wagon turned in with Connie and her son on it, she waved. Howard handled the team effortlessly and she made a quick note of that. When Jerry jumped down from the wagon, she sent him towards the stables to find Shawn first admonishing him to not go into the building or fenced in area without permission. She also warned him that there was a dog, but it wouldn't hurt him. Linking arms with Connie she took her up to the house. When Howard came back from dropping off the wagon and team, she asked him to bring tea to the library. "Well, what's new in town since I left?" She asked. "The shafts have all been closed. Mr. King had a meeting and told us that he'd reopen them and set the men to working on building houses, but we're scared. Some of the men are talking about

59

leaving to find another mining job but we hear they're scarce. For now, we're going to see what happens. We're no worse off than we were." The cook interrupted with a tray holding a steaming pot, two cups and a few cookies. She set it on the table and turned. "Connie," She exclaimed! "I didn't know you were who they sent Howard for." Then realizing she was talking out of turn she turned to Anne and stammered an apology. "Anne smiled, "No harm done, how do you two know each other?" She's my niece." "Well how nice to have family around. Does your sister live in town as well?" Cook shook her head and left. Turning to Connie Anne asked, "What did I say?" "It's ok" she said, "Mum died 10 years ago. She was one of the first to be sent away when the first shaft collapsed. " "I'm so sorry Connie, I didn't know" "You were only a baby then, it's ok" assured Connie. Once they had tea and munched on a couple cookies Anne explained that she was having some clothes made and the seamstress needed help. "Connie perked up when Anne said she'd be paid and that perhaps Sandy would take her on as a helper. "Lead the way Ma'am I'm ready to start now! I love to sew, and we need the money!" Anne showed her to the sewing room and left her with Sandy. She went to the nursery when she heard an argument going on. Shawn's voice was pleading with someone. Entering she found all 5 children gathered around a table.   Fiona was passing out milk and cookies, but Jerry was refusing to take any. Shawn ran to her. "My friend won't let me share my cookies and milk." He said breathlessly. "I told him it would be ok, even Fiona told him."   Anne smoothed back his hair and entered the room. Seating herself in the rocker she reached for James. "Jerry, don't you like milk and cookies?" "Yes Ma'am, I love them, but these are the big houses cookies and milk, and besides Mama doesn't have any." said Jerry. "Ah well, your Mama and I had our cookies already, but we had tea with them. She's going to be busy sewing for a while and I was hoping you could play with Shawn. You are welcome to cookies from the big house whenever you are here. Did you know your Aunt Jennifer made them? Now listen to Fiona while I go give this young man his morning snack." As she moved to the other room, she saw Jerry happily reach for a cookie and shove most of it into his mouth. Happy shouts of children playing interspersed with little squabbles that children have when they are fast friends rang through the house and around the yard for the rest of the morning. Anne spent the time in the library working on yet another list. When Sam came home, he found her there curled up in a chair with her planning face on. "Good afternoon wife" Sam sang out when he entered the room. "Oh my, I didn't realize what time it was. " Anne said hopping up and smoothing out the wrinkles in her dress. "I'd better see how the sewing is coming along and arrange lunch for them." "Them?" questioned Sam. "Yes, sewing for all of us will be a full-time job so I brought Connie up from the village this morning. That's her son Jerry out there with the children. Sandy will be employing her I believe. " "Wonderful" said Sam "I trust you asked her how the townspeople feel about the changes?" "Yes, we can talk about it after lunch if you like" replied Anne. Anne poked her head into the sewing room and was pleased to see the two women chattering away as they sewed. It looked chaotic to her, but she believed in letting experts do things their way and the two of them certainly looked like experts. "When you want to take a break luncheon will be served in the kitchen with the staff if you want." she reminded them. "Oh, said Connie "I'd better get Jerry, he must be hungry by now" Anne waved her away, "He can eat with the children. He had cookies and milk a while ago but I'm sure he's hungry now. " Connie thanked her and the two began folding up their work for a break. Anne joined Sam in the dining room and settled the children around the table. Jerry's eyes were huge as he looked around. "You have a room just for eating?" he said in wonder. "Yeah," lisped April "and another one for cooking even." The grownups smiled and Brian moved to serve the children. Fiona helped and soon everyone was munching away. There were a few slipups and one glass of milk took a tumble, but the meal was congenial. Afterwards Anne took the girls and James upstairs to settle them for a nap and Sam asked the boys how they planned to spend the afternoon. "Well," replied Shawn, "I have to go to the garden and fix the peas that Titan ruined this morning. Jerry can play with you though." I'm a little confused" said Sam "Who is Titan and why did he ruin our peas?" "Titan is what I named my dog and he got into the garden. I'm glad Bruce saw him when he did, or I might have to fix more than the peas." "I see.   Perhaps he needs some training? That's what Adam said. He said he could help me train him every day after breakfast. Gerald wasn't happy. He said I have to fix the peas even though I don't like them." Jerry offered to help and when Sam gave permission for that they headed for the garden with Shawn a bit happier that he didn't have to work alone.

Chapter 4

Setting Things Right

Sam went into the library to wait for Anne and started working on the store's books. Anne came in around two holding a piece of paper. "Brian gave me the list and I've arranged to start interviewing staff later today. Do you mind if I make some changes?" "Of course not, do what you see fit. I hope you plan to raise salaries for I doubt Mother paid anyone what they should be making." Anne handed him the list and he looked horrified. "No, it seems she didn't if this list is accurate and I'm sure it is. I've seen what is allocated to salaries every month and there is no way that is enough for all these people. It's a good thing we feed, house and clothe them as well. I heard from Gerald that she docked their salary every month for stupid stuff like breaking a dish or the tea not being hot enough. His got docked every winter because she felt he didn't have enough to do. She used to cut Bruce and Albert's in half in winter and make them clean the attic and basement. She got away with it because the food counted as part of their salary. I hope we can figure out everything she did and fix it. Anne patted his shoulder. "We'll make it right Sam. The staff will trust us enough to tell us what else has been going on soon. Calm again Sam inquired "Do you have time to talk about the town?" Anne told him what Amber had said about the concerns the men had and he agreed that they needed to have that town meeting very soon. They went over their agenda and Sam suggested he send Howard to post notices about it. "Sam, I know you mean well but you forget. Hardly any of the men read well and the women can't either. Schools were poor when I was a child and haven't improved. I wouldn't be able to read as well as I do if my Dad hadn't insisted we all learn" reminded Anne. "Thank goodness you are here to help me." Sam said. "I would have never realized that. We'll add an adult education program to the future plans. "Wait, all. Do you have brothers or sisters in town?" Anne shook her head sorrowfully, "No, most of them moved away when they realized the mines were their only choice. I hear from one or two occasionally. That's why the schools are kept poorly. When a child is educated, he doesn't want to work in the mines or pick up rocks and we lose them to another town with better opportunities. Perhaps we need to add that to the list as well." Sam nodded and explained he had arranged to go into work this afternoon since she would be doing interviews. He kissed the top of her head and left. Anne began perusing the list again as she waited for her first interview. The list gave name, job, age, and years with the family.

Brian	Butler	30
10 years		
Jennifer	Cook	55
5 years		
Howard	Dishwasher	14
1 year		
Fiona	maid, governess	21
2 years		
Harriet	maid	15
1 year		
Beatrice	maid	22
2 years		
Gerald	gardener	35
5 years		
Adam	groom	28
3 years		
Albert	gardener helper	16
2 years		
Bruce	gardener helper	16
2 years		

The list finished with a note.

She never told me about salaries, handled that herself. To be honest none of us really know what we make. Seemed to change every month depending on what went wrong.   We were always told that food, shelter and uniforms came out of our salaries. Since the Master died, we've been told that times are hard, and our Christmas bonus will be keeping our jobs. When he was alive things were different. His death stopped raises and other things.

After praying over the list Anne grabbed a pencil and began calculating salaries and benefits for everyone as well as what else was needed. When Brian announced her first interview, she was ready. Adam came in hesitantly, his hair slicked back but no longer dripping and his boots cleared of mud. Anne smiled and asked him to sit down. First, she checked to see that she had all the information correct as far as age, asked his salary and how long he'd been with the family. He told her he had a room off the stables that suited his needs. She asked if he had any plans for marrying since she was sure that room wouldn't be enough for a family and he explained that he had been married but she died along with his son several years ago. He doubted that he'd need more than his room. The barn had electricity he told her, so he was comfortable. Anne told him that a pony would be joining the menagerie out there and asked if he could give the children lessons. He said he had expected that and was looking forward to it. She asked if Sam had discussed her learning to ride as well. He said Sam wanted to teach her himself. Smiling, Anne asked if he needed help and he hesitated before denying any need. "Howard seems good with a team she commented, did you teach him?" Adam brightened up and said, "No, that boy has natural talent. He is amazing. He loves the animals and they adore him. Occasionally he stops in on his way home and even the goats crowd around him. " "So, said Anne, "If I were to make him a Stable Master's helper, you'd be alright with that?" "Adam smiled delightedly, "I'll teach him everything I know Ma'am. You'd be doing him a huge favor getting him out of the kitchen." "Well then we'll plan on that if he's agreeable. Please don't say anything to him until after his interview though. He's young so I want him to go to school as well. Can you work around that?" Adam nodded and then Anne explained his new salary, title, and benefits including the small cabin she planned to have built onto the stable in the back. Adam stammered, "I'm grateful Ma'am very grateful. You don't have to build me anything, I don't mind the room. " Nonsense" she said, "that room should belong to a stable hand not a stable master. You don't think Howard's parents will mind letting him live here do you?" "His father is gone but he needs to look after his mother." said Adam. "Leave that to me." smiled Anne. Checking her watch, she thanked him for his time and crossed one interview off her list. She had raised his salary plus meals, board, uniform with laundry services and a bonus for staying with the family when times were tough. As he left, she told him to send Howard in. Howard came in visibly nervous. The first thing Anne did was assure him he wasn't being fired. "I didn't mean to break the dish Ma'am honest." he burst out. "You can take it out of my pay just like before," Startled Anne looked at him. "Do you break many dishes?" "Oh no, I've only broken one other one. It cost me a day's pay" Anne frowned. "Well let's forget the dish for now. Tell me about your mother." Confused Howard hesitantly began. "Um she's fine. She's um nice. Err what do you want to know?" "Tell me what she likes to do maybe and if she has other children." "Mama likes to cook. She makes really good eggs when we can find them. I have a brother. He's 12. His name is Ben" Howard added. "He picks through the rocks." "I see. Alright Howard let's talk about your job. Do you enjoy washing dishes?" Howard shook his head hesitantly. "Well then would you mind if I changed your job?" "As long as I can still support my Mom, I'll do anything." "All right Howard I want you to become an assistant to Adam, the stable master. You'd be an assistant stableman." Howard stared at her. "You'd let me work in the stable, really? I can be with the horses? Will I make enough to support Mama?" Anne smiled at his delight. "Yes Howard, you'd make more than you do now, but you'd have to live in the stable. We're building a small area for Adam to live in and you'd take over the room in the stable. "I get to live with them too?" he squeaked "For real?" Anne laughed delightedly when his voice cracked. "Yes, Howard for real and I intend to bring your mother and brother here as well. He can take over your job and live with you in the stable room. You'll get your salary, room, uniforms and board but there's a catch. You must go to school. " Howard stared. He was speechless.   "I'll let you get used to the idea." She rose and called Brian in. "I think Howard needs to sit down for a bit perhaps with some milk and cookies?" He's had rather a shock. Also, would you send for his mother and brother please?" "Right away Ma'am. May I ask if he is still employed?" Anne nodded and he took Howard from the room. As he left Howard raised his hand in a small wave as if it was all he could manage at the time. Shaking her head Anne sat back down. Tears glistened in her eyes as she thought about how many of the staff expected the meeting to hold bad news and how grateful they were when she gave them what was only fair. Sam found her that way a bit later when he came in to get some paperwork. She didn't hear him come in and he studied her before realizing there were tears on her cheeks. Falling to his knees in front of her he took her in his arms and patted her back. "What happened? Did one of the staff say something to hurt you? I'll deal with them immediately." Startled Anne jumped when he touched her but then hugged him back. He released her and she sat up wiping her face. "No one said anything, it's just that they are so grateful for just a little bit of kindness. Howard could hardly talk when I told him he and his brother would be going to school and we would employ his mother. It is sad that they expect something bad when they come in here. Did you know your mother would tell them keeping their job was their Christmas bonus?" Sam shook his head sadly. "She has much to answer for I'm afraid. I sent her to a house I had rented with a couple servants. I'm going to have to go down there and deal with her soon." They linked arms and set off to find the children. After lunch the next day Anne went back to interviewing staff. The first person she saw was Howard's mother, Renee. Howard had obviously told her that she was to be hired as well as her younger son. The boy, Ben, stood awkwardly beside his mother. He did agree that dishes sounded better than picking up rocks in the hot sun. When Anne mentioned school however he frowned but his mother glowed. Assuring Anne that she was grateful she accepted the job as cook's helper immediately. Anne decided to talk to Brian about rooms in the servant's wing so she no longer needed to stay with friends and said Ben could share with Howard in the stable. After dismissing them to go collect their things she called Brian in. He explained that while there were plenty of empty rooms, everyone but cook had to share to save on heat. Shaking her head in disbelief she set that to rights. She decided to meet with the cook in the kitchen since the library seemed to be so negative for all the staff. Jennifer sat down at the table across from Anne after serving tea and cookies. Anne smiled. "Goodness you never seem to run out of cookies. and they are wonderful. I think you are a marvelous cook. I also think we are working you too hard. After all the household has grown in the last week and the servant's hall has more people as well." "I can keep up Ma'am I promise you don't need someone younger really. I need the work." interrupted Jennifer hurriedly. "Oh no Jennifer, of course you could but I think you deserve a bit of help. I've hired Howard's mother to be your assistant. I thought it might make up for me taking Howard away as dishwasher. He'll be working in the stables after today. His younger brother will take over as dishwasher. They'll both be in school as well. Perhaps your assistant can handle the breakfast dishes and he can do the others. Now your salary will of course be higher and when you have trained, I want you to start taking a day off every week. I understand you haven't been taking the half day you were allotted." Your salary will be raised, uniforms, food and shelter are, of course, provided as well.

You've been with us for five years which we feel deserves a bonus as well. With each statement Jennifer's mouth fell open further and further and she stared across the table. "Thank you, ma'am, I'm grateful, was all she managed to stammer out when Anne finished. Anne rose from the table after making arrangements to meet every Monday morning to discuss menus for the week. She went to the library and told Brian to come in. "Well, I am amazed at everything you have all put up with here, but I guess I know how scarce jobs can be. You've been with us the longest and we want you to have a bonus for that. Your salary is going up and of course uniforms, food and shelter are included. Now, why don't you tell me what is unfair here that I may have missed.?" Brian shook his head. "You've done a great deal for us already. I think we can ignore any inconveniences. Although I will tell you that stretching the servant's allotment of food may be difficult with the new hires." "Servants allotment?" inquired Anne. "Yes, we are allowed only so much food a day for the servants hall no matter how many people work here. The breakfast oatmeal stretches when cook adds water but the bread and butter for lunch can only be cut so thin. Dinner is leftovers but with 5 more people there really aren't as many leftovers to go around." Anne stared at him in shock and rang the bell for Jennifer. After a few minutes

Jennifer came puffing into the room obviously having taken the time to put on a new apron and wet down her hair. "Jennifer, first you needn't run when I call. If you were to slip on the stairs we'd starve! Second, I just found out about the unfairness of food division downstairs. From now on please cook the same thing including cookies and other goodies for the staff that you do for the family. If you need more help because of the extra work let me know. I want my staff to be healthy and that means good food and plenty of it. No wonder everyone is tired." Jennifer and Brian had huge smiles on their faces and after thanking her profusely Jennifer left. After thanking Brian for all his help, she waved him out of the room as he sputtered gratitude. Only a few more to go she thought and watched the maid enter. Harriot sat on the edge of the chair and kept her eyes downcast. The cookie Anne had insisted she take was clutched in her hand. "What are your duties here Harriot? "Anne asked hoping to put her at ease. "I um I clean, and I serve Ma'am, but I can do more if you want. I'm strong I can work hard" "I'm sure you are dear I don't mean to add to your duties, I just want to make sure they haven't been asking too much of you. I understand you do the basic dusting, mopping, tidying and serve at dinner?" Amber nodded. "Well I think your salary is too low for someone who does all that." At that Harriot risked a glance up wondering if she was being made fun of. It looked like Anne was serious. "Th th thank you Ma'am I appreciate it." Making a mental note to ask someone why the child was so timid Anne dismissed her after telling her uniforms, food, and shelter would be included. Brian ushered Gerald, Bruce and Albert into the room. Well let's begin with how pleased I am that the garden is going so well. I'm sure we'll be very busy canning this fall." Gerald and Anne talked about what it would look like to have the children helping and Albert added some comments here and there. Bruce was silent. Gerald mentioned that the twins had been working there for long enough that they knew how to do most things on their own and would be very helpful teaching the children. Albert nodded eagerly. Bruce smiled and nodded when Albert nudged him. "Bruce" Anne began. "I get the impression you aren't exactly thrilled with garden work." "Bruce sat up straighter and said. "Well Ma'am it's not my favorite but I'll do a good job I promise." Gerald agreed that despite his not enjoying the work he did do a good job. He also added that while the garden was large, he didn't need three people year-round to work in it. At that statement Albert and Bruce looked at each other nervously. Anne hastened to reassure them that no one was going to get fired. "Bruce," she asked. "Would you rather work indoors?" Bruce nodded carefully, not convinced that he wasn't about to lose his job. "Good" said Anne. "We need some extra help with the heavy work inside. Your duties will vary every day. You might have to help the cook with canning this fall, or scrub a floor, polishing silver would be your job and you'd train as a footman. How does that sound?" With each task Anne mentioned Bruce smiled wider and wider. "Thank you Ma'am I'll work really hard for you. I'd love to train as a footman and Albert wants to be a gardener." He turned to his twin. "Isn't it wonderful Albert? We each get to do what we love and we're still together like Mama wanted." After going over salaries and reminding them that uniforms, shelter and meals were included, she issued bonuses and ushered them out. Adeline, the laundress, came in looking tired. Her hands were red and rough, but she tried to hide them under her apron. Anne asked what method she used to wash clothes. The laundress explained that they had two large tubs in the basement that she filled with water and soda crystals and then stirred around with a pole. Stains were rubbed on a washboard. She then wrung them out and hung them to dry. Anne shook her head. Goodness, your workload must have doubled since we came. Adeline sat up straighter and shook her head. "It's ok Ma'am I don't mind I need the money. My husband was killed years ago in an accident and I stayed with family until the Misses let me come here instead of sending me away like they do now. I'm grateful for the work. I won't let the extra slow me down, I don't need much sleep." Anne sighed. "Everyone needs sleep Adeline. I want you to have more help. There are some widows in town that stay with their children. I think we should use one of the places my husband is building for a laundry house. You and however many widows you think can be supported by the business can work there. We'll send our laundry to you and pay a reasonable price for you to wash it. I suspect some of the unmarried miners will as well. That gets you out of the basement and should get you a bit more sleep. Of course, until it is set up we will continue to pay you and you can live and eat here. I'll make sure the building is roomy enough to hang clothes in the winter and has a drying line outside for the summer. Perhaps one with a second floor so you and your partners can live there. How does that sound?" Adeline stared for a minute then burst out. "Really? I can have my own business. That would be wonderful. I know two women who would love to move out of their son's houses and be independent again. I'll do a great job for you Ma'am. I promise. We'll work hard to make you a profit." Anne stopped her and explained that any profit would be theirs to keep. "We'll pay like everyone else does."

She promised. Beatrice came in next and perched on a chair. "I understand you are leaving us to get married in a week" "Yes Ma'am, I'm going out west to marry a man I've been writing too. His wife died in childbirth and he needs help with the baby. He seems nice." Anne could tell that she was nervous about her new life. She wished her well and told her if things didn't work out, she could come back. Beatrice shook her head. "No Ma'am I can't afford train fair back. I have to make this work no matter what." Anne handed her an envelope and said, "This might help with that. You can consider this your wedding present. Keep it hidden until you know if you'll be happy there. Also, when you are ready to leave Adam or Howard will drive you to the station with your things." Beatrice burst into tears of gratitude. Anne patted her shoulder and told her she and Sam would be praying for her. She then sent her to the kitchen for milk and cookies and went to find her children. When she reached the nursery, she found a young man seated on the floor with her children gathered around him. Frowning she looked at Fiona who sat in the rocking chair holding James. No one noticed her entrance they were so enthralled in the story. Listening for a minute she realized he was telling them about a train ride. The story abruptly cut off when they heard her clear her throat and the young man shot to his feet. Fiona put the sleeping James in his crib and came to introduce him. "It's my brother Miss Anne. He's here." "Yes, I see and with my children before I got to interview him. Come with me young man." Randall followed her from the room after glancing at his sister. "I'm sorry, they told me you were busy when I got here, and I couldn't wait to see my sister. It's been 2 years since I saw her." "Nevertheless, those are my children and I don't want strangers just going into the nursery." Anne said as they walked into the library. "What did you say about strangers in the nursery?" exclaimed Sam He rose to his feet and advanced to Randall who looked pale. Sam put his arm around Anne and whispered that he could take this interview while she checked on the children if she would prefer. "I do want to check on the children and speak to Fiona, but I want to be in on the discussion as well." she whispered back. "We'll wait for you." Sam replied, "It will be good practice for this young man." Anne turned to go hiding a smile at her husband's words. Fiona had the older three children coloring pictures when she walked in and after telling them to continue, she asked Fiona to come into the other room. "I didn't know you hadn't seen him yet honest." burst out Fiona as soon as the door was closed. "He just came in and surprised me. I'm so sorry." "I see. What can you tell me about your brother growing up?" "Oh, my he was fun to be around, but Dad almost wore out a belt keeping him in line. Once he climbed out a window to keep from doing chores and when he was old enough to go rock picking, he'd sneak away run back to school. He told the teacher he was sent there and made me promise not to tell. When payday came around Dad found out and well, he didn't sneak away after that, but he did make me tell him what the older kids were learning every night. I think that's why I did so well in school, I had to learn the lessons for him as well as my own!" "Perhaps you should be the teacher then." Smiled Anne. "No please, Randall needs the job. He worked so hard to get through Normal School. He mopped floors and washed dishes and anything they told him to do to earn his tuition." Anne sent Fiona back to the children and went to the library. There they found a very nervous young man standing just where she had left him. When she came in Sam rose from the desk and joined her on the couch. He indicated a chair for Randall who sat down looking as if his knees gave out as he did. "Well," started Anne. "Tell us about yourself." Randall told her basically the same story Fiona had told her, but he added an apology for not waiting. Sam glanced at Anne and at her nod asked, "Why should I trust you with my children when clearly you haven't shown good judgement? You influenced your younger sister to hold back important information from your parents and to do double work on your behalf." Why would I think you can influence young minds in a positive manner?" Anne chimed in. "Don't tell us that it benefitted your sister and therefore was excusable. She tried to plead your case that way already." Randall hung his head looked at them and seemed to come to a decision. "You're right I don't deserve to work with children. I did some terrible things that hurt my parents and sister and today I made another bad decision. But my last year at school I met someone who changed my life. He made me want to do better, to be better and to make up for the stupid things I did as a child and as a youth." Anne and Sam just looked at him waiting. "I met Jesus Christ. I know this household doesn't hold with religion, but He isn't just church or religion like I used to think he was. He is real and I only want to live for him now. That was why I couldn't wait to see my sister. I wrote to her as well as my parents when I became a follower and asked her forgiveness. She assured me that I was forgiven by all of them, but I had to see her to see how she would look at me to really know if she forgave me. I'm sorry." Sam and Anne asked him to wait outside while they talked. "I do rather believe him." Said Anne. "And he obviously isn't aware of the managerial changes that have taken place." Sam nodded. "We can hire him, but I want it understood that he is on probation and that he is not to be alone with the children in the classroom. I'm also going to work on that school building a bit harder. Is there one of the staff that can take lessons with them?" Anne nodded. "I've already told Howard and his brother to be there. I think Howard would tell us if any plans were made that we wouldn't approve of. He'd at least tell his mother and she would tell us. " Sam found Randall outside the door respectfully standing about 3 feet away so he couldn't have heard anything that was said. He asked him to come back in and Anne explained his duties and that he would have a room in the servant's area. They agreed that since the children were quite young lessons would be held for only a couple hours in the morning. When he asked what he was to do the rest of the day. Sam replied. "You'll be teaching the staff to read and write. Skip Latin but add in history and some basic math skills. Lessons will be after lunch for 3 hours every day. Oh, and while in the past this household may not have followed Christian practices, I hope you find my wife and I have changed things. Your day off will be Saturday and you will be expected for Church on Sunday along with the rest of the staff. I hope you enjoy working here." He called Brian in and asked him to get him settled in the room next to his. And Randall, I want a list of materials you'll need for each group you'll be teaching. Brian after you get him settled please call an all staff meeting in the main dining room for a half hour from now." He turned to Anne and said. "I think we need to present a united front about Sunday morning and afternoon lessons. What shall we do about the children while we hold our meeting? Anne offered to be with the children but was pleased when Sam said he wanted her there. "Fiona can read and write quite well." She reminded him. "She'll be exempt from the lessons. She also already knows that she's expected in church on Sunday. Perhaps she can skip the meeting I'll go explain it to her." "Good" Said Sam. "And ask her to have the children ready for an outing when we're done. I have plans for us this afternoon!" "No more spoiling I hope" Anne smiled to show that she wasn't too serious as she turned to the stairs.

After everyone but Fiona was gathered in the dining room Sam started by apologizing for the food shortage that had become standard practice there. He assured them that they were unaware of the traditions and that it would change immediately. Anne explained that they wanted the staff to join them at church Sunday mornings. Sam went on to explain that sometimes he and his wife would be too busy to meet with them daily to give tell them any changes in orders. They would be setting up a small mailbox in the kitchen where they could check to see if anything changed for them. Brian and Jennifer don't have time to read everyone their notes so all staff would be expected to learn to read and write. Class would be held here in the formal dining room every weekday afternoon from 2 to 4. Math would also be taught along with some history. The younger members of the staff would be receiving their lessons with the children in the classroom in the morning from 9 to 11. He added that anyone who learned enough to pass the eighth-grade examinations would of course receive a bonus. He introduced Randall as the teacher, and they suggested he get started finding out what instruction everyone would require immediately. He then requested Brian and Jennifer come with them to the library. As Brian closed the door, he turned to them. "My wife just informed me of the situation in the kitchen and you have my abject apology. I had no idea my mother has been so tyrannical with the staff all these years. If there is anything else, we need to fix please don't hesitate to let me or my wife know. We'd also like to know if anyone has a problem with taking lessons. We feel it is important for everyone to learn to read and write but we don't want anyone to feel put down or awkward." "No Ma'am." Said Brian. "I think you handled that very well.

Separating the children from the adults will help a great deal. I think everyone is pleased with the changes you've made. I apologize for Randall slipping past me today. I was called away when the new dishwasher broke a dish. I thought he'd stay in the hallway where I told him to wait." Anne nodded and asked. "Why would they call you for a broken dish?" Cook replied. "So, we would know how much to deduct from his salary. Different dishes cost different amounts and I while I don't do the buying, I can record it." Sam opened and closed his mouth several times and finally turned to Anne who carefully replied. "I appreciate that you are so conscientious with our funds, but I think we can excuse a broken dish or two when someone is just learning his job. From now on just write me a note what dish was broken and who broke it and if it becomes a recurring problem, I'll handle it. Thank you." Sam and Anne looked at each other in amazement then hurried up the stairs to see if everyone was ready for their trip. Fiona had everyone shined up and coats on when they came in. "Come with us." invited Sam. Fiona hurried into her coat as well. Sam picked up James and led the way down the stairs and out the door to the stable. "Ohh, do we get to see the horses again?" Amy asked? Adam was waiting with the wagon hitched up and the back padded with plenty of straw. He tossed each child in making them squeal in delight and assisted Fiona into the back as well. Sam handed her James and helped Anne onto the front bench. Waving vigorously the children bounced around as Sam drove them down the lane. He leaned over and told Anne that he would be teaching her to ride while the children had lessons starting next week. Anne almost squealed in delight herself at that but managed to keep it to a delighted grin. After about an hour Sam turned into another farm and pulled up by their barn. He lifted Anne down and stood at the back of the wagon. "Anyone who can tell me the rules here can get down and come with us. If you can't remember them, you'll have to stay in the wagon." Shawn spoke up first. "We have to stay out of the barn unless a grownup is with us and we can't go through the fence or even the gate unless we have permission. Permission has to be spoken in a sentence, so we know you mean us." Sam nodded and lifted him down. April pointed to the gate and fence and lisped, "No No." She then pointed at the barn door and repeated the words. Amy piped up. "I'll hold her hand, so she doesn't forget to ask before we go into the barn or fenced in yard." Sam smiled and said, "Who'll hold your hand?" Amy stretched up as tall as she could and said, "I'm a big girl. I can watch her. Behind her Fiona nodded so Sam lifted them both down pretending to drop them so they would squeal again. He took James and handed him to Anne and helped Fiona down. Taking both girls by the hand she walked them over to the fence where they could see several horses and ponies munching on grass. Shawn was already there staring at the animals. Shawn guided Anne up to the barn with his hand at the small of her back. When they got close a tall man came out and shook his hand. He tipped his hat to Anne and tapped the baby's nose. Glancing over at the children lined up at the fence he asked. "Want me to have my son take them for a pony ride while they wait?" Sam left it up to Anne. After hesitating she nodded. "One minute" he said and ducked back into the barn. Shortly a young man led a buckskin colored pony into the corral. He opened the gate by the children, but they didn't move. Looking confused he asked, "Don't you want a ride?" April looked up and yelled "Senense you need a senense."Shawn moved past her and grinning. "Sentence was what she said. We're not supposed to go into a corral unless a grown up tells us it's ok in a complete sentence. I think what you offered would do though." Sam ducked into the barn before the kids would see him laughing. He was almost suffocating himself in an effort to keep it in. Anne just smiled and walked beside him. "You need more practice keeping a straight face." She told him. Breathing heavily Sam agreed. "And I know just

where to get it!" While they were talking the owner
of the farm walked out holding the halter of a
chestnut mare and a dun mare. Anne was enthralled.
immediately handing James to Sam, she didn't hear
another word Sam, or the man said. She carefully
pet both mares and fed them the carrots Sam handed
her. The men sat down on some hay bales and
watched her get acquainted with the horses. The dun
soon realized that she was out of carrots and
wandered off, but the chestnut stayed nuzzling her
and accepting Anne's hugs. "Well, I think that
decides it. We'll take the chestnut." When he said
registered, Anne turned to him. "What do you mean?
She's beautiful but much too big for the children."
"Not too big for you." Sam answered. "Me?" Anne
turned back as the mare nudged her complaining
about the lack of attention. "Me?" "She could be
mine?" Sam smiled. "She is yours. It is my wedding
present to you." Adam will teach you how to ride
her, but I think you already know how to make her
happy." Anne threw her arms around the horse and
squealed in delight. The man shook his head.
"Haven't heard noises like that since my kids grew
up. Enjoy her and I'll have my son drop off the pony
and cart on Monday if that's alright." Sam shook his
hand and headed out. "He can pick up the bridle then
as well." After he tossed the reluctant children into
the wagon, he helped Fiona in and handed her

90

James. The horse was tied to the wagon and when Anne tried to climb into the back of the wagon, he steered her to the front and helped her onto the seat. Anne kept looking backwards the whole way home. When they got there Adam came out and looked over the mare. Turning to Anne he asked, "What do you call her?" "Does she have a name?" she called to Sam who shook his head. "He sells so many horses that he doesn't name them, just gives them a number. She's number 675 but I doubt she'll answer to it." He explained. "Guess you'll have to name her." "Ohhh," breathed Anne. "Can we call her Spice?" Adam nodded and took her to the barn. "You can call her anything you want my dear. I'm glad you like her. Now let's go get dinner, I'm starved." The children seemed to feel the same way for they ran for the house. By the time Sam had pried Anne away from Spice they were upstairs ready for dinner. Sam led Anne into the formal dining room and seated her at the table. "After dinner I'd like to read to the children if you don't mind." He said. Dinner was wonderful, much less rich than the night before but wonderful. There was still dessert but not the rich chocolate cake they'd been served last night. After dinner he curled up on the rug in the nursery with his favorite book from childhood. When he looked up he saw 4 pajama clad children with eyes riveted on him. He began reading aloud. He smiled when he closed the book at the end of the chapter and discovered that Shawn and Amy were the only two still awake. Anne and Fiona were as entranced as the children. He promised to read more another time and told Shawn to be sure and catch up April and James since they had fallen asleep.   He scooped up the little ones one at a time and tucked them in bed kissing them on the forehead. Then he tucked Amy and Shawn into their beds and did the same. He told Anne he'd be in the library and left. Anne knelt by each child's bed and smoothed the covers. When she got to Shawn, he opened his eyes. "Mama I don't know what to do. Mr. King is really nice, and he does all the things Daddy used to, but I don't want to call him Daddy. He's not my Daddy, but he is. What should I do? He looks hurt when I call him Sir and he's a grownup so I can't call him Sam." Anne took a minute to smooth Shawn's hair back. "Your right darling. He isn't Daddy but he is your new Daddy. I think he loves you children. Perhaps we can come up with a name for him that isn't Daddy. He was friends with your father and Daddy would want you to honor him. What about Papa? It means the same thing and we never called Daddy that." Shawn smiled sleepily. "Papa, thank you Mama I knew you'd have an answer. "A few minutes later Anne entered the library smiling. Sam was hard at work redoing the agenda for Sunday's town meeting. They had decided to have it after church since everyone would be together anyway. The agenda they had planned grew until it included everything from kittens to mine safety. Anne wrote it out in her beautiful script.

Safety

Houses

Company Store

School

Feral dogs

Vermin

Chickens

Retired Miners

Widows

He offered her the mine safety report that he had received from the expert, but Anne said she'd read it later. Summarize it for me for now. "Well, we have some shoring up to do in 2 and 3. 1 needs some major overhaul which makes sense since it is the oldest. They think it may not be worth fixing so we must decide if we should close it or not. 4 will need to be redug completely and 5 is going to be started next week. The rock pile has kids climbing all over it and they are concerned that someone may lose their footing and fall. We really don't make much profit from picking rocks and I want the kids in school so we're going to close that part of the operation and level the pile. It will stay where it is for gleaning. If we close 1 then we can fill it in with the debris, so children don't go exploring. I understand there was a cave in many years ago and I thought we should put up a notice with the men's names on it as a memorial." "Perhaps we can put a memorial in the cemetery instead. That way people won't be tempted to explore the mine." Anne suggested "And include all the men whose bodies have never been recovered." "I like that." Sam agreed. With the agenda set talk turned to inconsequential things and suddenly Sam asked. "Would you like a desk? In here I mean. We're partners and it doesn't seem right that I sit at the desk while you sit in the chair like an employee." Not giving her a chance to answer he said. "Of course, you need a desk. What have I been thinking? I should have done this sooner. I'll have one brought in tomorrow." Anne blinked. "All right if you would like to. I'm sure I can use one. I rather think we could share that one though. Take turns sitting in the chair maybe?" With that she rose and wished him pleasant dreams. As she left, he called out. "Oh Anne, I have to go take care of a problem tomorrow so I will be leaving early." She waved her hand in acknowledgement and continued up the stairs. In the morning Sam rode Sugar into the closest town with a train depot and traveled to the town his mother was living in. He arrived at the house just after lunch. His mother was finishing her coffee on the porch. Seeing him she immediately launched into a tirade about how neglected she'd been and how few servants she had here to take care of her. When she started in on Anne, he stopped her. "Enough, you may complain about me all you want but you will never say a negative word about my wife or children. I've been talking to a few people and I know what you've been doing to the poor people that work here. I considered doing the same to you for a time but have decided that sending you off in a wagon with a couple crates of belongings because you're too old to make me a profit wouldn't be the Christian thing to do." His mother gasped and tried to tell him she had done everything for him, but he stopped her again. "No more. I don't believe anything you say so don't try. You had one child because it fulfilled your obligation to my father. You fought to take over the reins of the company because you thought he was wasting money so much you sent him to an early grave. Then instead of telling me I had inherited everything when I turned 21 you took over and ran the company like a dictator of a small nation. Your reign is over. I will not turn you out, but you are going to go where you will not make trouble for anyone ever again." His mother fell silent and stared at him. "You're just like your father." She burst out. "Thank you." replied Sam. "It wasn't a compliment." she returned as she rose to leave the room. When she reached the doorway, she stopped and turned back. "Why are those trunks being brought down the stairs?" "You are moving Mother. You wrote me complaining about the accommodations here at this house, so I am giving in. You don't have to stay here." His mother straightened up. "Well, I'm glad you came to your senses. I won't share a house with that hussy though. You'll have to send her and the brats back to town." I told you not to insult my family. From now on every time you say something negative about her, I will arrange for you to travel further west and to live in a smaller town. For now, I have rented a house in the country for you. It's in Tennessee. If you cause trouble there or try to cause trouble in my household, I will put you in a home for people who don't have the mental capacity to live alone. I intercepted the letter you wrote to Anne. If you try to contact her again, I will have you declared mentally incompetent." His mother paled and reached for a chair. "You wouldn't dare!" She shouted. "Oh yes, mother I would. Remember I am not just the child of my father I am yours as well. I would dare in fact I have already started the process. I may have forgotten to mention that you will have a companion or two at this country home. Ones I am paying well to keep track of everything you do and report to me each week. Your days of tyranny are over for good." He went outside and sat on the porch and waited. A few minutes later his mother came out even angrier. "I suppose this is part of your plan as well. That maid won't listen to me." "No, she won't." agreed Sam. "I gave her a bonus to not listen to you. Perhaps your people would be more loyal if you paid them better. Which reminds me I don't want you to have the burden of hiring or firing help anymore. And I wouldn't want you to sully your hands with money either. Your companions will be paid by me and any expenses you have will go through them. They are well trained and well paid. You are welcome to try to change their ways, but it will be fruitless." A car pulled up then and a couple got out. Sam went to greet them and then introduced him to his mother as her new personal servants. He turned to leave, and she shouted. "Wait, what about my footman, I'd hate to see him lose his job, he had an old father to support." "Ah yes I forgot to tell you. He is in jail for theft. He's been stealing from you as well as the townspeople for years. His father is with him. Now, good day mother, feel free to keep in touch." "Doesn't it say something in that Bible you set so much store by about honoring your mother? Do you feel this is honoring me? I'll be like a prisoner." Sam looked at her. "Why yes it does. I love you and I am honoring you. I am providing for your comfort and safety. I've even arranged activities for you to take part in if you choose. There is a church you can walk to that had many things available for the local elderly. Penelope there will be glad to take you any time you choose or if you prefer Adrianne who is waiting at the farm can take you. I am making sure you are safe 24 hours a day. A doctor is on call if needed and the house has many amenities including a full library. If you choose you can enjoy your remaining days. The cook has all your favorite recipes and there is a cleaning service that will come in once a week. If a situation occurs that requires strength or a man's touch Jasper will be there to take care of it. You will be well taken care of mother, just will be prevented from causing any more trouble. Feel free to introduce them as your companions or family, whatever makes you feel most comfortable. Now if you'll excuse me, I have a story to continue reading to your grandchildren and I must catch the next train to get there in time." With that Sam began walking back to the train station whistling happily. When he got home, he went straight to the nursery. When he walked in, he was mobbed by the three that could walk. It seems the pony had been delivered. The little ones hadn't realized when they were playing with it that it was going to be theirs to keep. Looking around he asked where Anne was. Fiona laughed. "She is out in the stable still. Spice was delivered also. I'm surprised you didn't see her." Sam smiled. "I left poor sugar tied out front. I'll go unsaddle him now and see if I can drag her back for story time. While I'm gone you all figure out a name for that pony." Sam ran down the steps and headed for the corral. He led Sugar into the stable and cross tied her. As he brushed his horse, he listened to Anne singing to Spice in the next stall. Glancing around he saw Adam seated on a bale of hay just inside the stall keeping a close eye on the new horse. When Anne realized he was there she rushed to him startling Sugar a bit. After apologizing to the horse and giving him a bit of carrot, she started telling Sam how wonderful Spice was. Adam came out then and offered to finish putting Spice to bed. Catching her before she could go back into Spice's stall Sam turned Anne towards the door. Assuring her that Spice would be there in the morning he walked her to the nursery. If he hadn't told her that James needed to be fed, he was afraid she might sleep with the horse. When they got to the nursery Anne took James in the other room but left the door ajar so that she could hear what was going on. "Well?" questioned Sam. "Who is living in my stable? The children all tried telling him at once, but he was getting better at discerning words so this time he got most of it. "Ok what I am hearing is that you want to name him something that goes with Sugar and Spice. Is that right?" April spoke up then. "I wanted to name him Pony, but nobody liked that name. Shawn said we should name him Coal 'cause that's what makes our money." Sam smiled and looked at Amy. "What do you want to name him little one?" Amy crawled into his lap and said I want to name him Mine 'cause we have a mine." Sam looked at the children. "Those are all good names, but he can only have one name. Perhaps we can come up with one that means all those things." Anne spoke up from the next room. "What if we called him Penny? It sounds like pony and we get pennies from coal and our mines." "No" burst out Shawn indignantly. "That's a girl's name!" Sam looked at him and he settled down and apologized to his mother for sounding rude. "How about Copper?" asked Sam. Pennies are made of copper and that's not a girl's name. He's even kind of copper colored." The children enthusiastically embraced the name and started making plans for a name plate on his door since he couldn't wear a collar like their other pets.

Chapter 5

The Meeting

The next evening Anne and Sam drove down to the old schoolhouse. They were silent mostly, each wondering how the townspeople would react to the changes about to be implemented. Everyone had already gathered. The woman and children seated at the desks and the men stood in the back and along the sides. Sam took Anne's hand and moved to the front of the room where he seated her in the teacher's chair. It occurred to him that perhaps he should have faced everyone alone or at least come better armed for safety. Standing at her side. He began by thanking everyone for staying under his mother's rule and apologized for not seeing what was happening and taking over sooner. He promised to make improvements and to listen if there was something the men needed. A shout came from the back. "Talk, it's all talk" The men began murmuring angrily. Anne rose and pushed Sam aside. He had immediately stepped in front of her in fear that someone might throw something but as soon as she rose the men fell silent. "Stop. You haven't heard our plans yet. My Donald would listen. You know he would. Sam was his best friend growing up. So, I ask you in his memory to listen to what we have to say. I don't want to hear anymore shouting Barney. If you have something to say, then say it but after you have heard us out." Anne then took Sam's hand. Startled Sam looked at her. "Please go on husband." Anne gave the crowd a warning look and then sat back down. Sam began again. "First of all, I want to talk about mine safety. You all know the expert from university was out here yesterday. He gave me a list of suggestions on what we can do to have four safe mine shafts. He also suggested we close down number 1 because it is about played out." Whisperings grew and Sam hastened to assure them that it wouldn't result in a loss of jobs because he was opening another shaft. Everyone listened quietly while he explained what needed to be done to each shaft. When he mentioned throwing the rocks in the mine to close it one of the younger teens jumped up. "Wait," he yelled. "I need to work. Are you going to let me in the mine then?" Sam looked seriously at the young man. "We have a plan so that no one will lose the income they have now. Can you be patient like the men are until we are done talking to ask your questions?" One of the men came forward and leaned down to whisper in the boy's ear. Looking reluctant the child sat back on the floor with the other boys. "Now." said Sam "I'm leaving a list with each shaft manger. He will divide up duties with you so that the work gets done as quickly as possible. Remember the sooner the shafts are safer the sooner we can get back to work. Number 4 has no manager since Donald was killed so I'd like to appoint one now." Pausing he glanced at Anne who was giving him rapt attention. She nodded encouragingly. "The new mine manager will be Charles. I want to see all four of the shaft managers tomorrow morning at the house to discuss how to proceed. I also want an election held within each shaft group. One man needs to be elected by his coworkers to represent you. While we are willing to listen to any of you, I think it would go faster if one man from each shaft came to a meeting every month to discuss anything we might be missing. I expect elections to be held tomorrow evening when each shaft group will be having a separate meeting. Their first duty will be to report on that meeting to me. The next item on our agenda has to do with housing. Some of you men have been building houses. We hope to divide you all up in the next few weeks, some on houses, some on stores and some in the mines. I've heard some of you are wondering who gets the new houses. I can't think of a fair way to decide so we'll have a lottery. You may have noticed that some of the houses are larger than others. I don't know how you women have been able to raise children in the small tinderboxes my mother provided. I am impressed. The lottery will have to take in account who has more children and the larger places will go to them. Now before anyone asks, after all the new places have been built the old ones will be torn down and rebuilt as well. Eventually everyone will be in a new house. I ask patience while we build. Your husbands are working as fast as they can!" Murmurs came from the woman then, but everyone settled down quickly when Anne rose. "I was one of those women just a few short weeks ago. I know how hard it is to raise little ones in what was basically a large box. Your men may have told you these new houses, which you will all get, will have rooms. The largest will have two or three bedrooms upstairs, one-bedroom downstairs, a kitchen and a large gathering room. While we will own the houses, you will be able to make or buy furniture for them if you wish. We will build a storehouse to hold the furniture that is available to use rent free, but you won't be required to use it. Decorate as you want. We will make available everything you have now but there will not be a limit of one bed or two spoons as there has been in the past. You may borrow as many as you need for your family. All we ask is that you keep the houses

105

in good repair as well as our things if you choose to use them. If you leave our town you take anything you own with you." Anne sat back down. Sam smiled proudly at her. "That brings us to the third thing on our agenda. "The store. You may have noticed that Cyril, the former manager, has been replaced. The new manager, Cecil, has been busy going thru the records. He informs me that many of you have been cheated over the years. Price gouging and exorbitant interest seemed to be the way things went. That is over. Prices will be set to still make a profit, after all Cecil and his family need to be able to make a living, but if you find that prices are set much higher than stores in other towns I want to know. I realize that woman do more shopping than men, so Anne has agreed to meet with the wives of our four shaft representatives each month. Please let her know of any problems with the store. I believe Cecil is a fair man. He has turned over all accounts receivable to me. Almost all of you owe the store a great deal of money. I believe that some of you had money withheld from your wages each week to pay it off. I find very little evidence that anything has been paid off in the past, however. Here's what we've decided to do about that. Anne placed a kettle on the teacher's desk and Sam ripped the pages from the account books and threw them into it. He then struck a match on his boot heel and threw it in as well. Everyone stared as the records went up in smoke. "I think you have all paid enough. Please don't feel this is charity. It isn't. Wilber and my mother wrung every penny they could out of each slice of bread your children ate, and I am sure those accounts are more than paid in full. Now the next item on my list may not be popular with everyone here but I ask that you hold your comments and questions until the end. I have asked the state to fire the schoolteacher. I spoke with many of you about the quality of education your children have been getting and I found it lacking. He didn't teach enough for your children to read a book or to figure out a total at the store. I want that to stop. I have made arrangements with the state for a new teacher and he starts Monday. The school will teach reading, writing, history, math, science and spelling thru the 8th grade level. Any child that tries should be able to pass the examination for high school. I want all your children from age six thru twelve in school every day. Mr. Newton has agreed to teach the younger children in the morning and the older ones in the afternoon. School will be held Monday thru Thursday. Your children will bring home schoolwork as well. Please give them time from their chores to do it. On Friday he will be setting up 2-hour sessions for anyone over the age of 12 who wants to learn. He will work around your shifts and I hope you woman will help each other out with childcare so all of you can get whatever education you desire. I won't require you to attend but I will say that the ability to read and do sums will help you get ahead in life. The shaft managers will be appointing shift foreman and they will have to be able to read, write and have some knowledge of math. Anyone who wants to learn can, but it is only compulsory for the youngsters. Our children will be attending as well." Anne again rose and took over the meeting. "I know that some of you who live far from here don't send your little ones to school because of the danger involved in walking thru the field. The feral dogs attack and some of you have lost children to them. I told my husband about it and we decided that they must be done away with. I don't care if you poison them or shoot them or find another way to get rid of them, but every dog killed from that pack will earn you a bounty. Now." Anne turned to where the teens were mostly sitting on the floor. "I don't want you going out to find the dogs and kill them without an adult. Those dogs are dangerous, as dangerous as a mountain cat would be and they run in a pack. This isn't a lark. This is serious. Don't go out alone and don't under any circumstances go out after dark unless an armed adult is with you." Just as Anne finished lecturing the impulsive teens a scream was heard outside. The men rushed out, but Sam vaulted out a window. The full moon revealed several dogs snapping and jumping at a girl who was trying to defend herself with a walking stick. The men rushed forward but before they got to her a shot rang out. Freezing they turned and saw Sam revolver in hand taking aim again. Two more shots rang out quickly and the fourth animal ran away towards the woods. A man picked up the sobbing girl and carried her back to the schoolhouse. When everyone was inside again. Anne inspected the child for bites while her father stood watching. "Why did you come Hannah? You know the dangers." The young girl sobbed out, "Mama, Mama is having the baby. We need the doctor." Sam sprang into action. He handed his reloaded revolver to her father. "Can you shoot?" he asked. Nodding, the man looked at the gun in his hand and turned to the others. "Caleb" he called, "can you get the doctor?" "Take my horse it'll be faster." offered Sam. "Suzanne can Hannah stay with you?" As the woman nodded, he turned, but then he turned back "Thank you Sir I'm grateful" At that he ran for home. Sam and Anne turned to the folk who were left. She looked at the teens, hoping they got the message that no one was safe alone and unarmed. "I have a couple more things I'd like to talk about if you can stay another half hour." Everyone settled down and the meeting resumed.

Taking a deep breath Anne continued. "One of the other problems we've had are the vermin in the houses. No matter how clean we kept things we couldn't get rid of mice and such. I believe I've found a solution that will work and not cost us much. In fact, at first, I don't think it will cost us anything. Our stable has no mice. I was quite surprised at that until Adam showed me why. We have wonderful little mouse catchers. We'd like to share with you. I want the children in charge of this. We are giving away kittens. If you take care of them, they will gladly take care of the mouse problem in town. Right now, we have five of them. Next week I understand we may have a few more. But there's a catch. I don't want to be down here next year discussing a feral cat problem. These kittens are to be pets. They won't require much food. Any child between 6 and 12 can choose a kitten. You must have your parents' permission and parents you must agree that they will have a place in your home." The children in the audience were grinning and had started begging the closest parent for a kitten. Clapping her hands Anne quieted them down and promised that they would take names at the schoolhouse next Wednesday. "That gives you three days to convince your parents to let you have one. In addition to the cats, we'd like to know if anyone would be interested in chickens. After the feral dogs are gone, we'd like to have one or more of you volunteer to raise chickens for eggs and meat. We have enough animals at the house, but we do need eggs. Perhaps some of you would be willing to provide us with eggs in return for our buying chickens. Of course, you can sell any surplus of eggs or any that don't lay well. We wouldn't expect free eggs for life of course, just until the initial cost of the chickens, feed and fencing was covered. Let me know next week when we woman meet who is interested." She glanced at the teens as she said that and several of them seemed interested in the idea as well. Sam stood beside her and said, "That is everything on our agenda." I'm sure you all have questions. Let's try to be orderly about it. One woman raised her hand hesitantly and Anne nodded at her. "I was just wondering if you'd be open to something besides chickens?" At their look of confusion, she rushed on. "I was raised on a farm. We had a small herd of cows. I know how to take care of them and thought perhaps with little ones you might need milk at the house." Sam looked thoughtfully at her. "I don't know what is involved in raising cows but if you can come to the house and give my wife and I some more information next week we can consider it." A man rose in the back. He stood holding his hat in his hand looking down at his feet. "I don't like to admit it, but I know I'm not the only one here who depends on his son's income from picking rocks to get by. It sounds like you are doing away with that job." "Yes." Sam said "We are. However, I feel there are other ways your son and any others can make extra income if it is needed. Selling eggs is one way, the store will be hiring clerks, we'll need young people to help in other ways as well. I wasn't going to mention this until I spoke with the shaft managers Monday, but I've visited some other mines in Pennsylvania and talked to the owners about what they've been paying their miners. I'm sorry to say our pay scale is one of the lowest around. We plan to fix that. The average salary of a minor starts at around 2500.00 a year. Most of you have been at this many years longer and make far less. We'll be raising salaries to compete with other mines. It will be dependent on how long you've worked for us and what your particular job is, but no full-time employee will have to depend on their son picking rocks any longer. Your shaft manager will have a meeting with each of you to discuss salaries after our meeting Monday." Anne stood up at this point and added, "Some of your children are supporting their mothers and I know you are worried right now.   While there are no mine jobs available to women right now there are other jobs if you want to work." Looking around the room Anne spotted Connie and Jim. "Would you two come to the house tomorrow morning to talk with me about jobs for woman and men who don't have someone in the mine working please?" Another man stood. "We were wondering why you are making us leave that big field alone. We heard you were going to have us fence it." Sam nodded. "Yes, I almost forgot. That field is being set aside for gardens. Any of you who would like a plot to grow fresh produce is welcome to use it. We'll appoint someone to take names and divide up the land so everyone that wants to can grow vegetables." Several others had questions which were answered in turn until suddenly Caleb burst into the room. "It's a girl." He yelled and everyone began talking and milling about. Caleb handed the pistol back, and Sam turned to Anne. "Ready to go? I would assume if Caleb is back then the wagon is hitched up and ready to go." They quietly made their way thru the room answering questions and greeting people as they went. Once outside Sam helped Anne onto the seat and got up himself. Taking the reins, he sighed. "Wow a baby and a dog attack, is it always this exciting down here?" Anne just shook her head. "Usually exciting here means surviving until payday." As they rode home Anne's head dipped lower and lower until it rested on Sam's shoulder. As he drove, he prayed that someday she'd see him as her husband and thanked God she was willing to be his partner for now. When her reached home he picked her up and carried her up to her room. She woke up as he opened the door and looked startled. Setting her down on the bed he kissed her forehead and left. Dropping to her knees sleepily she thanked God that Sam had been so understanding these past few weeks and that someday she'd be ready to be more than his partner. The next morning four women climbed the slight hill up to the house. Connie and Jim were with them. Anne was waiting for them on the porch. There was a tray with seven glasses of lemonade and seven fresh baked cinnamon rolls sitting on the table by her. The conversation was polite and stilted until Anne said, "We've known each other for years, we've visited back and forth and watched each other's children play. You stood with me while they tried to save Donald. I'm still the same person. Yes, I live in a bigger house, but I haven't changed. Can you please not look at me as the wife of the owner and see me as Anne, the woman you grew up with?" The four women relaxed a bit at her words and talk turned to the night before. They told her about the baby born. The little girl was doing fine and the mother while tired was as well. Talk turned to the meeting and one of the women asked if she thought the changes would really happen. Startled by the question Anne replied, "Yes, of course. Sam gave his word. They

114

may not happen all at once, but they will happen. Some of them already have. You saw him burn the accounts. You've seen the men working on new housing. We had a man and his family visit last night that wants to start a store here to sell what Cecil's place doesn't. He plans to stock furniture and kitchen things. Cecil wants to focus on groceries, so he'll be giving up the other parts of his store. Sam is looking into having someone start a fabric store or a clothing store. So yes, the changes are coming, even more than we mentioned last night. Sam is determined to make things here better than any other mining town and he is spending a great deal of money to do it. He wants to make up for the years his mother ruled. Now, who is unable to work in the mines that she didn't run out of town?" The oldest of the woman pulled out a list and gave it to her. There were three woman who had stayed although they lived with other families. There were four men who were too old to go into the mine that lived with their children's families." Anne perused the list thinking about possible ways for these seven people to earn a living. She promised to get in touch with all of them as soon as she could with possibilities of jobs. She told them about the laundry starting up. They figured that would take care of two women. One man had already been hired as a guard and one found a place at with the new storekeeper. Talk turned to children and husbands the way it always did when friends got together. As they left Anne told them they were welcome to visit anytime. They set the first Saturday of the month as the date for their next meeting. Entering the house, she headed for the library to jot down notes from the meeting but as she got closer, she heard laughter coming from the room, Sam's the loudest of all. Peeking in she saw them all on the floor surrounded by books and making silly gestures. Fiona was in a chair by the door doubled up with laughter. When Anne entered the three oldest ran to her all talking at once. She could hardly understand them. Finally, she raised her hand for order and said, "Giraffe, elephant? Sam is the lion? Whatever are you talking about?" Fiona quickly filled her in. "Acting Ma'am, they've been acting out the books as he reads them. It's ever so funny." "I see, perhaps you should show me." The children ran back to Sam. Amy yelled "Papa Papa Mama wants to see you be a giraffe." Stunned by the name Sam stared at the children. "Yes Papa," Anne said gently. "Let's see you be a giraffe" I'd rather be a big big bear." Sam cried as he grabbed all three in his arms and rolled around the floor with them. James cried out from his place on a blanket. He rolled over and got up on all fours. This was his newest trick to get attention. When that didn't work, he pushed of and began slowly making his way across to join in the hilarity. Everyone stopped and held their breath as he figured out how to crawl successfully. Finally, Anne couldn't stand it any longer and swooped him up into her arms laughing. "How clever of you my sweet. Your crawling. Nothing is safe any longer is it?" Sam stood and joined her. James reached for him and he took him in his arms. Tossing him into the air and catching him soon had James laughing happily. The children gathered around excitedly chattering about James being able to play with them soon. Lunchtime came then and they all went off to the dining room. Shawn called lunch their manners practice which made the adults smile. Fiona went to have lunch with the staff. She enjoyed her hour of adult conversation every day. Today lunch was a beautiful cheese souffle, toast points and lemon cookies for dessert. Fiona came and collected her charges for washing up and naptime. Sam invited Shawn down to the library while the others napped. When the children were gone Sam turned to Anne. "Papa?" he queried. "Yes. Shawn realized you didn't like them calling you Sir and asked me what to do. He didn't want to call you Daddy since he remembers Donald so well and we came up with Papa. Is that all right with you?" "All right? It's the best thing that I've ever been called in my life! It took every bit of self-control to not break down when she said it. I've never been so happy!"

117

Anne smiled. "I have to talk with cook this afternoon about next week's menus. Amy's birthday is coming up and we need to talk about that as well. What do you and Shawn have planned?" "A birthday? You'll have to give me dates for all the children and yours as well. Let's talk about that this evening instead of business since it's Saturday!" Sam held Anne's chair as she stood up and smiled at her warmly. "You are beautiful you know. I love the color blue on you."

Chapter 6

The Hero

He went to the library and knelt to put books away. Shawn came in and began to help him. "Thank you, son. " Sam said when they were finished. "I'm glad you pitch in where it is needed without my having to ask. Now let's go for a walk. I'd like to see your garden and perhaps pay a visit to the stable to see how the new horses are getting along." "May Titan come too?" asked Shawn. "He won't get in the way; I've been training him." "All right" said Sam "I'd like to see what progress you've made there as well." The two walked outside and Shawn gave out a shrill whistle. Titan came bounding up from the stable running and tripping as only puppies with big feet can. He skidded to a stop in front of Shawn and sat down. You could tell sitting was very hard for him. He was wiggling around and quivering with the need to jump up and greet his master. Shawn praised him and pet him. Sam leaned down and pet him as well and was rewarded by a quick slurp across his face as his reward. Laughing he tousled Shawn's hair and grinned. "Did you teach him that?" He teased. Releasing the pup from his sit position Shawn giggled. They started walking to the garden fence with Titan running circles around them. When they reached the fence, Titan sat down and watched them enter the gate. "Impressive behavior." praised Sam. "You've done well." "Adam and Gerald helped me." Admitted Shawn. "Glad to hear you are giving credit to them as well Shawn it is the kind of thing a man would do." Shawn was showing off his neat rows of vegetables when they heard the pup yelp. Sam ran thru the garden and vaulted the fence. A dog from town had come into the yard and attacked the friendly pup. Bella came running low to the ground and bowled the interloper over. Sam grabbed Titan and tossed him over the fence to Shawn. "Stay there" he yelled as he circled around trying to get a shot in without hitting Bella. Suddenly he heard a shot behind him and whipped around. Gerald and Adam stood there each armed with a shotgun. Looking in the direction they were aiming he realized that there was a pack of five dogs running to join the fight. There had been six, but one was on the ground motionless. He turned back to the fight and saw Bella was holding her own. Moving closer he saw his chance and fired.   Immediately turning to the rest of the pack he saw only one left and Bella was headed for it. Quickly he dispatched the beast and called Bella to him. He checked her over for bites but found only scratches. Gerald and Adam picked up the bodies and disappeared in the direction of the field. Sam opened the gate and found Shawn seated on the ground holding Titan. Sam sat on the ground beside him and asked to see the puppy. There was only one bite mark on him, and it would heal. Reassuring Shawn that his pup should be fine he took the boy in his lap. "That was terrifying wasn't it?" he asked quietly. Shawn looked up in wonder. "You were scared Papa? You didn't look scared." Sam gathered the little boy close to him. "I was terrified. I was never more scared in my life. I was afraid one of the dogs would jump the fence and get to you. I was afraid your mother would come out onto the porch and the dogs would attack her. I was afraid for Bella, and I was afraid six dogs were more than I could handle without getting badly hurt. I was so thankful to see Gerald and Adam were armed. You see Shawn, " He continued. "Courage isn't never being afraid, it is being afraid but doing what needs to be done anyway. It's waiting to cry until the crisis is past and you've done everything you can to fix the problem." Shawn looked up at him. "Thank you for saving Titan Papa. Do you think he'll be the same after this?" "I think he'll be a bit more careful when he sees another dog after this. I think we've all learned something. Now I hear Bella whining outside the gate. I think she wants to check her pup over as

121

well." Shawn put Titan down outside the gate and Bella was all over him in an instant. Closing the gate Shawn looked for Sam and found him on his knees trying to repair the damage his boots had caused when he ran for the fence. Without another word Shawn ran over to help. They were still there when Gerald and Adam came back. Gerald praised their efforts. and the four of them walked to the stables. Sam thanked the other two men for coming to his rescue. "We were standing in the field looking at the goats and talking when Bella burst out of the stable and ran for the front. She was low to the ground, so we knew something was up. We were talking about going rabbit hunting, so we were armed. I can't imagine what might have happened if we hadn't been." explained Adam. "Me either" agreed Sam. "Have the dogs ever come up from town before?" "Not that I know of" said Adam but I heard about the bounty so town may be too hot for them and they are widening their territory. We'd better keep a close eye on" He stopped there realizing Shawn was listening to every word. Sam nodded. "I've hired a guard for the yard and we'd better bring the goats in closer to the stable. I wish we had room to keep them inside at night. You two split the bounty on those six dogs and I'll buy you ammunition. Can you stay armed as you work around at least until the problem is alleviated?" The men agreed and Sam and Shawn began to walk back to the house. Bella had taken Titan into the stable room with her and they left her for now. On the way, "Shawn asked if they were going to tell his Mom about the attack. "I think she should know, don't you? Sam asked. "We want her to be careful if she goes outside." "That's true" said Shawn. "Perhaps we should tell Fiona as well since she is outside with us a lot. Let's not tell the girls though. It will scare them." "Well it might but I'd rather they be scared and careful than have no idea the dog in the yard might be dangerous." replied Sam. "Plus the shots may have awakened them. We'll do whatever your mother thinks best." Anne was waiting for them on the porch. "I thought I heard shots." She said anxiously. "What happened." As they explained her face grew pale. Sam insisted she sit down and sent Shawn for a cup of tea. "He explained about the guard and that he would be teaching both her and Fiona how to shoot. Shawn came back at that point and asked if he could learn as well. Anne started to say no, but Sam put his hand on her arm. "Of course, we can teach you as well son, and we'll have some gun safety classes for your sisters as well. Now go see if everyone is awake yet please." He turned to Anne. "I'm sorry if I overstepped just now but he needs to learn. The girls too. They will be around guns here and I want to know they are safe with them. " Your right of course, I'm just having trouble thinking of him as growing up, but he'll be nine soon." said Anne. Sam pulled her to her feet and hugged her. "Don't worry" he said. "I won't get him a rifle for his birthday ... yet. And I convinced him to let you tell the girls about today's incident. They have to know not to go near stray dogs." A few days later the children were playing outside. Fiona was trying rather unsuccessfully to make sure James didn't crawl off the blanket. The retired miner Sam had hired was sitting near them rifle in hand. Suddenly he rose and shouted "Run!" The children looked up and saw three dogs running towards them. Shawn urged the girls towards the garden fence. Fiona grabbed James and ran with them. The guard, Bert, started firing. He dropped two of them. Anne ran out onto the porch with another rifle but as she started towards the garden another dog came around the corner of the house and charged her from behind. It grabbed the arm with the rifle, and it flew from her grasp. Bert immediately ran for her, afraid to fire for fear of hitting her. Moments later the dog decided he was the bigger threat and released Anne to attack him. She grabbed her rifle and killed him. Panting they looked around the yard. Bert yelled there's another one somewhere. As the words left his lips, they heard Fiona scream and a shot rang out from the garden. Seconds later they had the gate open, but the

124

dog was lying on the ground dead. Shawn was holding the baby and the girls were gathered around Fiona crying. The rifle that Gerald kept on high hooks in the garden was on the ground. Anne took James while Bert replaced the rifle making sure it was loaded and placed it back onto the hooks. Gathering all his charges he suggested they go back to the house before any explanations occurred. Once inside they gathered in the library. Anne thanked Fiona for saving the children and she shook her head. "Wasn't me Ma'am. I didn't know Gerald kept a rifle there. I had just closed the gate when that huge brute jumped at it. It startled me and I fell to the ground. I was holding James and it made him cry. Then I saw it clear the fence like it was nothing. I rolled over to protect the baby and I heard the shot. When I sat back up Shawn was reaching for his brother and the girls ran to me for comfort. I thought one of you had done it." Anne looked confused. "Then who ..." As she started to speak Bert grabbed Shawn's hand and shook it. "Quick thinking lad, you saved your family today. Your mother and I couldn't have gotten there before someone was badly hurt." Anne stared in shock. "Shawn? you fired that shot?" "Yes Mama. I know I'm not supposed to touch a gun unless you or Papa tell me to, but you did say unless it was an emergency and that dog was really big. Bella would have gotten it if she wasn't out with

Adam and Gerald taking the goats to the other pasture. Am I in trouble?" Anne burst into tears and grabbed the little boy. "Trouble? you are amazing. I'm so proud of you I don't know what to say. Your father would be so proud too. And Papa will be thrilled as well. I think this calls for a celebration. Let's see if Cook has time to make one of her special chocolate cakes for dessert tonight. You and I will go ask her while the others head for the nursery for a story." Bert slipped out while they were talking intending to go bury the dogs. He found Adam and Gerald loading them into a wheelbarrow. He told them the story and they shook their heads amazed at the child's quick actions. Bella circled around them growling at the contents of the wheelbarrow. "That explains why Bella was in such an all fired hurry to get home." mused Adam. "Just before we heard the shots, she took off running." "That's when I realized I had left my rifle under the overhang in the garden. I thought I'd hear it from the boss, but I guess I'm not in trouble now." Adam said as they headed for shovels and the far pasture. "That's 13 of them. How many more can there be" asked Gerald. Bert grunted. "Last time I heard the pack had split. That big un led the larger of the two packs. It had about a dozen in it. The other pack only had six or eight." Adam did the math. "So, there's still at least another half dozen out there somewhere. Let's see if the boss will let us go hunting tomorrow. We need to clear these out once and for all. They must have a den on the outskirts of town. Maybe even some pups. Let's get them before they hurt someone." Sam came home late that night. Dinner was over and he thought the children would be in bed. He slipped into the library quietly and sat at the desk. Then he realized Shawn was sleeping curled up in the chair Anne usually sat in. He quickly went to him and picked him up intending to tuck him back in bed. Shawn woke up and grabbed his neck burying his face in his shoulder. Changing direction Sam sat in the chair cuddling the boy. "What's wrong son? Are you sick? Has something happened to your sisters or Mother?" Shawn sat up and rubbed the tears off his cheek. "I made Mama cry today. I didn't mean to." He choked out. Sam rubbed his back. "Want to tell me about it Shawn? Was she mad at you?" Just then he heard someone running on the stairs and Anne burst into the room. "Shawn's not in bed and I can't find him anywh..." Her voice trailed off when she saw them. "Oh Shawn, I was so scared when I saw you were gone." Anne fell to her knees in front of them hugging her oldest. "I'm sorry Mama, I had to talk to Papa, so I waited for him." Shawn hugged her back. Sam rose still holding the child and helped Anne to her feet. Keeping one arm firmly around her he led them to the parlor and seated them on the couch. "Ok, here we can all be close, and someone can tell me what happened while I was gone. Words poured out of both at once and Sam shook his head. "All I could get from that was dogs and rifle. So, I am assuming that we were attacked again. I am guessing everyone is fine since no one led with that news. Shawn how about you tell me what happened first and then your mother can fill in any gaps." Shawn told him about running to the garden and the dog coming over the wall. He hung his head when he told of grabbing the rifle even though he knew he wasn't supposed to touch it. At that point Sam tucked his finger under the child's chin and lifted it until they were eye to eye. "Am I to understand that you saved your sisters and brother from that beast?" When Shawn and Anne nodded, he went on. "You have nothing to apologize for. You did everything right. Yes, you broke a rule but sometimes a man must weigh rules and duty. We have a duty to protect our family and if that means a rule must be broken then so be it. God's laws come before man's rules. You made the right choice. I'm sure it was terrifying, and you showed great courage. I am extremely proud of you. And Shawn always look someone in the eye when you speak to them even if you are confessing a wrong." He turned to Anne and asked her where Bert was that the children were in danger. Her quiet reply of "Saving me" caused him to set Shawn beside him on the couch and scoop her up into his lap his eyes searching her for injury. She laughed and assured him that she was fine. She told the part of the story that Shawn couldn't see from inside the garden and when she reached the part about the dog coming around the house, he took her arm and ripped the sleeve to examine the bite. Shaking her head, she scolded him for wrecking the dress and explained that it wasn't bad Bert was there before the dog could get a good hold. Not convinced, he insisted on seeing the wound. Anne showed him then went to recover it. "I'll be back with some refreshments in a few minutes. Don't go anywhere." While she was gone Shawn climbed back onto his lap. Sam looked down at him and explained. "Do you remember when I told you courage is doing what needs to be done and reacting to it later?" Shawn nodded. "I almost didn't have time to be scared but afterwards I sure was. April wet her pants she was so scared." Sam covered his laugh with a cough and continued. "Well Moms are like that too. She was scared but showed courage. Afterwards she cried because she was so scared. She wasn't upset with you; she was proud of you and relieved that nothing worse than wet drawers came of it." Anne came back in carrying a tray as he finished. "Oh darling, were you worried that I was crying? I'm so sorry. I was just so glad everyone was

129

safe." Shawn hugged her and then looked at the tray. "I already had cake tonight Mother. but Papa didn't. It was really really good. Cook made it to celebrate everyone being safe. We saved a piece for Bert tomorrow." He still eyed that cake. Sam took a piece and winked at Anne. "It's a shame you already had a piece." He said as he took a bite. "Perhaps one more bite wouldn't hurt since you were so honest and told us you shouldn't have any more." He traded bite for bite until the piece was almost finished. Shawn was practically sleep in his arms and didn't notice when Sam ate the rest of the piece. Lifting him Shawn carried him up the stairs and tucked him back in bed. Anne was waiting for him in the library. Sam poked his head in the door. "Let's go talk in the kitchen so I can see if there was anything to go with that cake, shall we?" Anne jumped up. "Oh my, I never even thought, I'm so sorry. I can fix you a plate." Sam smiled, "Doesn't matter, I've wanted to eat dessert first since I was younger than Shawn. Finally got to!" Laughing they went to the kitchen where Anne found dinner in the warmer for him. They discussed their days while he ate and together, they washed up the few dishes they had used. Together they climbed the stairs and at her door Sam kissed her forehead and hugged her wishing her a good night. The next day Gerald and Adam along with several men from the village who had been released from their building commitment for the day went looking for the pack of dogs. They found them and removed the threat. As they were leaving Gerald stopped and cocked his head. "Did you hear that" He asked? All the men stopped and listened. They followed the noise to a tree and found that there was a den dug out under the roots. In it were five small puppies. "They aren't even weaned yet" said one of the men. "Bella is still nursing her pups once in a while, I'll see if she'll take to these." said Adam as he gathered the little balls of fur into a bag. "Anyone want one when they're old enough?" The men promised to talk to their wives about it. When the two men got back Adam whistled for Bella. She was very interested in the contents of the sack he laid by her nursery box. As soon as he opened it, she removed each pup and led them to her brood. Laying down she allowed them to nurse and then thoroughly bathed each one with her tongue. Adam nodded. "Well guess that answers that question." he thought to himself. Sam gladly paid the bounty on almost two dozen dogs including one to a delighted little boy who had never had money of his own before. Sam offered to take him shopping but Shawn told him he was saving it for a rifle of his own when he got older.

Chapter 7

Christmas

Several weeks went by and finally the houses in town were ready for their families. By then thanks to Sam's efforts town had a furniture store, a grocery store, a fabric and dressmakers store, and best of all a doctor. School had started and the adult education classes were popular. The church was built, and a new minister expected any day. The minister who married Anne and Sam retired and he and his wife went to live with one of their grown children. The pups had new homes where they were learning to protect their people instead of attacking them as their parents had. The kittens had grown to be terrific mousers and the vermin problem was way down. The mines were declared safer and ready to be reopened and the men were receiving much fairer wages. A system had been put in place to mentor the newer miners so that they learned how to stay as safe as possible in the tunnels. Sam was receiving weekly letters from his mother's caregivers that all was well and even got a letter from his mother that didn't accuse him of destroying her life. The harvest came and went. Cecil sold out of sugar and salt several times over as the women canned their garden bounty. The men took the time to hunt as well and salted their catch for winter meals. Things were looking up for the town of Hope. Christmas was almost upon them and Anne and Sam were having planning sessions almost every night. Jennifer and Anne met several times to discuss goodies that needed to be made. Sam discussed Christmas with his managers, and they came to a fair agreement. They decided to give each family a live turkey. Cecil sold them to Sam at cost and made arrangements for the head of each household to pick them up at the store. Several families decided to not butcher their bird so that they would be able to raise a flock. Anne talked Sam into playing Santa Claus after the Christmas Eve program and they gave out candy sticks to every child. The children had put on a wonderful program planned by the minister's wife. There had been a school program also, so the children were looking forward to a week of rest before having to go back to lessons. Anne kept Howard busy putting together wreaths from fresh pine boughs he had cut and sent the children out with Gerald to cut down a tree. They decorated it with strings of popcorn and ribbons and bows. Sam bought a few glass ornaments as well and the children carefully hung them. After Snow tried to climb the tree, they banished the kittens from the parlor. The girls protested that and wanted Titan banned as well but the dog hadn't broken anything so could stay. Sam commissioned Bert to carve a nativity scene with goats and horse, kittens and dogs. He finished it a few days before and the family set it up in the dining room. Anne laughed at the kittens and dog but loved it when Sam explained to the children that God loved all animals not just the ones that were there when his son was born. After a great deal of whispering, presents were picked out or made and carefully wrapped and placed under the tree. Christmas Eve before the stockings were hung. Sam called everyone including staff into the formal dining room. He read the Christmas story and led them in prayers for the new year. He thanked each of them for bearing with them during the transition and turned to Anne. We wanted to give you all a small gift to let you know how much we appreciate your work over the last year. She then handed out a small box of candy to each staff member. Every male member of the staff received a new pair of Jeans and a flannel shirt while each female was gifted a new dress. In addition, they each got a handkerchief from the children. Anne had helped them pick out a pretty one for the women and a nice bandana for the men. They explained that the children did extra chores to earn the money to buy them, so the gift was truly from them. The staff was amazed. This was the first Christmas they could remember being given a present since Sam's father had passed away. Jennifer then brought in refreshments and everyone sat talking until the children started to fall asleep. Sam woke them up to hang stockings and then he and Anne tucked them into bed. "This is the best Christmas ever" mused Anne. It was so hard to teach the children to give before. There was almost no money to set that example and they only got gifts made from worn out aprons or sticks. Now they are eager to earn and see it as a privilege to make gifts for people. Thank you, Sam, for making this possible." Sam hugged his wife. "You and the children have made me happier than I ever was before. I should be thanking you." I think I'll sleep in the parlor tonight, so I see their faces when they come downstairs early in the morning." Anne laughed. "There is no need for that. Go sleep comfortably. We will see that they wake you up stockings in hand tomorrow morning. Speaking of which we'd better go fill them!" Walking softly, they retrieved the socks from the mantle and placed some candy in the toe, oranges in the heel and a small package in the top. Cook came in with some gingerbread men to tuck into the very top of each. She had thoughtfully made James' gingerbread out of a teething biscuit so there wasn't a choking hazard. She had also made some small very soft candies that wouldn't stick in his throat. Anne hugged her for the thoughtfulness and wished her pleasant dreams. She suggested that the children might not need breakfast in the morning and suggested Jennifer sleep a bit later. Whispering goodnight to Sam Anne took the stockings upstairs with her. As soon as she was gone Sam tiptoed to his room and got her presents out of his top drawer. He had wrapped them earlier. They looked a bit less pristine than the ones Anne wrapped but he'd done his best. He tucked them under the tree and then quickly fixed a stocking for his wife in much the same way they had done the children's. He ran down to the kitchen where he found Jennifer waiting for him gingerbread man all ready for the top. Smiling he blew her a kiss and went upstairs. What he didn't know was that he just missed Anne coming out of his room sock in hand. She tiptoed downstairs and engaged in the same activity Sam had just been doing complete with what she thought was a secret trip to the kitchen where she found Jennifer waiting to give her the gingerbread made for the top of the stocking. Anne smiled her thanks and tiptoed up to bed. Jennifer shook her head and then finished the gingerbread men and placed one on a plate at each staff person's place along with an orange. She left a note that lunch would be the first meal served on Christmas. Then she climbed into bed without first setting her alarm for the first time since she'd been hired. Old habits die hard though and the next morning found her up first as usual. Since she had time, she made a batch of biscuits and gravy to supplement the gingerbread breakfast. Then she started stuffing the turkey which was where Brian found her when he came down. Shaking his head in disbelief he wished her a Merry Christmas before going to raise the rest of the staff. Hmm sniffed Jennifer as he left "You wouldn't have been able to sleep in either!" Upstairs the children were starting to wake. They knew it was Christmas, but they weren't super excited until they went to wake their mother and found her waiting with the stockings in her hands. Telling Fiona to get a bit more sleep she led them to Sam's room. She sent Shawn in first to make sure he was dressed and then opened the door. Sam woke up when three children pounced onto his bed. James was doing his best to wriggle out of his mother's arms to get to him. Laughing he sat up against the headboard and accepted his stocking from Anne. He whispered something to Shawn who excitedly ran to the easy chair, retrieved his mother's stocking and handed it to her. Anne smiled at Sam and sat at the foot of the bed. Gingerbread men were gobbled up quickly and wrapping flew as the children opened the present they found in their stocking. Shawn was surprised to discover a pen knife. He got off the bed to open it and admire it. Sam told him that he was never to open it unless he was three feet away from people and that Bert had agreed to give him lessons in carving. Amy and April received their first piece of jewelry. They were tiny pearls on a slim chain. Anne put them on for the day but explained they would stay in her room so that they didn't get lost. James was trying to eat the wrapping paper, so Sam helped him open his present. It held a wooden ring. It was sanded smooth and he promptly put it in his mouth and bit down on it. Anne smiled and picked him up. "What a smart boy you are. You knew just what that was for didn't you." At the children's excited urging Sam and Anne opened their stockings. Sam had a pair of mittens for his gift which he promptly put on. Anne gasped when she opened hers. It held a beautiful pearl necklace. She put it on, and her eyes glowed even as she scolded Sam for spoiling her. Sam pulled out his pocketknife and peeled 5 oranges. Shawn sat by the door and worked on peeling his own. Sam noticed him wince once or twice but remembering his first time with a knife decided to not say anything unless Shawn did. Anne luckily didn't notice. She was busy making sure James didn't choke on his orange. After everyone was thoroughly sticky and the candy had been discovered and devoured, they trooped to the nursery to wash up. Sam promised to join them in a few minutes. Throwing on clothes after washing his face he hurried in to find A water battle going on. Anne and James were not in the room, so he figured James was finishing his breakfast in the other room. Frowning he quickly turned off the water, handed out towels, and pointed to the puddles on the floor. The children weren't used to him being in the role of disciplinarian and hurried to obey him. When the room was dryer, he urged them into clothes and settled them at the small table to color while they waited for Anne. When she came out, he took James from her so that she could get dressed and turned to the crib. Placing him in it he changed the diaper and then tried to put the wiggling boy into some clothes. The other children left their coloring after a minute and came to watch. Soon they started offering advice and Sam got a bit frustrated with the Mother does it this way or Fiona does this when she dressed him. Stepping back, he looked at the little one grinning at him with one sleeve on and started laughing. Hearing a soft giggle behind him he turned. Anne was trying very hard to not laugh at him but wasn't being successful. She looked at him. "Don't worry by next Christmas he'll be more cooperative!" Then she stepped in and had the baby dressed in 2 minutes. Handing him to Sam she suggested they go sing Happy Birthday to Jesus.

They all went down to the dining room. After singing Sam quizzed the children to see what they remembered of the Christmas story and was pleased that they could tell him most of it. Cook came in and offered biscuits and gravy, but no one was hungry. "Let's go see the tree again." Suggested Anne. The children ran to the parlor where they found Brian standing in front of the closed-door arms folded across his chest. Skidding to a halt the children formed an orderly though crooked line and waited. When their parents got there. Sam moved to the front of the line and cautioned them not to run. He handed James to Shawn and he and Anne slipped through the door. The children strained to peek but couldn't see anything. After giving them a few minutes to get settled, Brian opened the doors wide allowing the children to see. They stood there for a few minutes staring. There were presents under the tree! It was the first time they had ever seen presents under their tree. Usually stockings held the only gifts. They only froze for a minute before they came hurrying in. Shawn handed James to his mother and headed for a red wagon sitting at the side. It had his name on it. The girls were kneeling in front of a dollhouse with April's name on it. Beside the house was a box holding little furniture and a small doll family with Amy's name on it. They quickly decided to share and started playing happily. Anne set James down next to a box of blocks and he grabbed the tag with his name and tried to chew it up. Laughing Sam sat down next to him and showed him how to stack blocks. When he was sufficiently distracted, he stole the slimy tag and held it out to Anne. "Oh no, I'm not touching that thing." She said. "You're on your own!" Laughing Sam crawled to the wastebasket and after a few tries managed to shake the thing off his hand. Then he rose and handed Anne a box with her name on it. She touched her pearl necklace and looked at him. "Only fair darling. We agreed to give them three presents each just like the Christ child received from the kings. So, you get three also. You don't want the kids to grow up thinking adults don't get presents, do you? That wouldn't make adulthood look like much fun would it?" Anne shook her head and took the box. "You come up with the greatest ideas." She commented. Opening the gift, she found a hand carved jewelry box. "Oh" she gasped. "It's beautiful. Did Bert make it?" Sam smiled smugly. "No, he didn't, I did. Bert may carve more than I do but I haven't forgotten the lessons he gave Donald and I many years ago." Then it was Sam's turn to open a present. He found a scarf to match the mittens that were in his stocking. "You've been busy." He commented and leaned in to kiss her cheek. He called the kids over and reluctantly they lined up in front of him. "Who

141

knows about the wise men?"   he asked. The
children knew the story although April had a very
hard time with the word frankincense and Amy
called it more not myrrh. Since Jesus got three gifts,
we decided to give you three gifts as well this year.
How many have you gotten so far? "Two" they
yelled together. "Well we'd better make that three."
he said pulling five wrapped packages out from
behind him on the couch.   The tree older children
eagerly tore open the gifts and found small leather
belts. They looked them over confusedly and then
saw each one had the name of their pets burned into
the leather. "Collars" they shouted and turned to put
them on the animals. Titan was in the wagon and
accepted his collar happily. The kittens were a
different story. They were happily playing with the
wrapping paper and trying to knock down James's
blocks. It took a bit of corralling but eventually all
the animals were sporting their collars and the
children were playing again. Anne handed Sam his
third present and he found a hat to match the scarf
and mittens. Smiling in delight he promptly put the
set on and handed Anne a small box. In it she found
a Cameo. "It was my grandmothers" Sam explained.
"I thought you should have it." "It's beautiful"
whispered Anne with shining eyes. "You've
thoroughly spoiled me." "Then I've done my job."
Replied Sam. James had given up on the blocks and

crawled over to the couch that Sam and Anne were seated on. He pulled himself up and stood easily one hand on her knee. For fun Sam moved to the floor about three feet from the baby and held out a small present. It was brightly wrapped and caught James' eye immediately. He reached for it, but Sam was too far away. He switched hands but still couldn't reach it. Hesitantly he put one foot forward. Anne caught her breath as he let go and balanced carefully. Sam smiled even wider and shook the package. It rattled and James' stared at it. He put the other foot out and then another. He teetered precariously but regained his balance and took a third step falling into Sam's lap package in hand at last. He had learned from watching his brother and sisters that something better than the wrapping paper was inside and tore open the gift. Inside was a wooden horse just the right size for pudgy fingers to grasp. Sam looked up at Anne. " How 'bout that honey. James gave us a present! The morning passed quickly with the children playing and the adults talking quietly. Lunchtime came and the girls were reluctant to leave their dollhouse, but Anne insisted. After lunch they found that Brian had moved the dollhouse and furnishing upstairs. Anne placed the jewelry box on her dresser and made the girls put the necklaces in it before nap. "Anyone who takes a nap gets to play outside." said Sam as he closed their door. Shawn

143

looked up at him when he said that and frowned. Sam tousled his hair and whispered, "and anyone who is over eight years old." He sent him out for his first lesson with Bert who was waiting on the porch. By the time Anne was done nursing James, Sam had cleaned up the wrapping paper in the library. They sat talking comfortable together. Sam offered to walk down to the cemetery with her after the children woke up and she thanked him for being so thoughtful. We went yesterday while you were working. I didn't want them sad on Christmas. "I would have gone with you if you'd told me. I want to be there for the sad times as well." Gently admonished Sam. "Next time, on his birthday we'll all go." Promised Anne. "When are you going to see your mother?" She asked. Sam groaned. "Do I have to? I'm kidding of course. I sent her a present. I don't think she'll miss me. Christmas was never a big deal after Dad died. I don't have good memories." "We'll fix that." Said Anne as she leaned over and kissed his cheek. "Now, I hear little footsteps so gear up for some outside fun." The children burst into the room all bundled up. Anne grabbed her outdoor clothes form the closet and called Shawn to come play too. They went outside and made the most of the snow in the yard. Sam and Shawn were wrestling with Titan and Bella when they realized the girls had disappeared.   They followed their footsteps around the side of the house and were pelted with snowballs. A quick retreat didn't help because the girls had made lots of snowballs and Anne was carrying a load of them in her scarf. Sam was laughing so hard by the time they ran out of ammunition he was almost short of breath. He finally rushed the little girls scooped them up and dropped them into a snowbank. Cold, soaked but happy they went inside dropping wet things on the porch. Jennifer was waiting for them with hot cocoa and cookies. Fiona had towels for all of them. The children came to the dining room for dinner that night. Cook served an amazing dinner. There was roast turkey, fragrant stuffing, mounds of mashed potatoes, vegetables the children had grown in the garden, rolls that almost melted in your mouth, and homemade pickles. For dessert there were four different kinds of pie, cherry, apple, blueberry, and a creamy chocolate custard. After dinner some very sleepy children were tucked in and prayed with and over. Christmas that year had been a rousing success.

Chapter 8

Hope

The new year dawned clear and bright. The children made resolutions and colored pictures to show what they planned to change in the new year. As usually happens with resolutions they were broken by the end of the week. Sam took the opportunity to explain that only with the help of Jesus can we truly be changed. The children prayed with him and tried again with a bit more success. When they failed now though they knew why and prayed for help to change. Everything seemed to be settling down. The mine was producing, stores were making a fair profit and the town folk were enjoying their new prosperity.   Then Sam got a letter from the union. The United Mine Workers had formed a couple years ago and for several years his mother had been giving lip service to the union. She made them the same empty promises she had given Sam. Abigail had worked very hard to prevent a union representative from coming out to the mine but Sam invited one so they could see what he was doing to make improvements. The representative wanted to make Sam pay back benefits when he heard the conditions the men had been working under prior to his taking the reins. The men refused to allow that. They threatened to not join the union if he did that. Sam was now giving them more than the UMW felt was fair and allowed them a voice in many decisions. They said it would eventually even out and to leave them alone. Wages had been given according to the suggestions made by the UMW before, but now there were fewer deductions. Price gouging was a thing of the past and families could actually start saving. In addition, they got vacation time and paid holidays. The mines were safer and there were jobs available for those who didn't want to work the mine. Holidays were real instead of being just on paper. The town was growing. Sam had worked very hard to bring in other businesses and made improvements to the school. Children were learning and had a chance to go on to high school if they wanted. Adult Education classes were slowly filling up as everyone realized that it would give them better opportunities. They got 4 holidays a year. Easter, Christmas, New Years, and the Fourth of July. He had also started giving vacation time depending on how long the men had worked for him. After a year they got three days. It went up a half day every year after that. He put a cap on it at 3 weeks. The union man went away shaking his head over the changes. He agreed that someone would

come back every six months to see if conditions
were being met or not.

Sam and Anne thought it was time for a party. When
they bought up the idea of a town wide party
everyone got excited. They'd never done anything
like that before. One of the miner's wives suggested
that they finally name the town since it had become
more than just a store and miners houses, and
everyone embraced that idea as well. The
storekeeper eagerly offered to keep a list in his
window of all the suggestions that were made.
Voting was set for the night before the party. The
woman got together and decided what food to serve.
Sam suggested he judge a baking contest, but they
just laughed at him. Someone suggested booths and
the furniture store owner offered to build several
from the crates he and Cecil got deliveries in. Sam
got in touch with the farmer who sold him Anne's
horse and he agreed to bring a couple ponies for the
children to ride. Adam offered to bring some of the
goats down for a petting zoo and mentioned that the
pups would be ready to be given out by then. He
also suggested they bring Bella to show what a dog
could do with some obedience training. Sam asked
him to consider teaching a class on how to care for
and train a young dog sometime after the party and
he agreed. The party rapidly became a fair. April

called it "Name Day" when they were talking, and it stuck.   Name day plans were talked about after church and anytime more than two women were together. The party had become a fair. Who would give speeches was discussed and what they could sell at the booths? The four women who represented each shaft took the reins and planned the event. They met every week and divided up the work. One woman could not take on the major job of coordinating food but one headed that project while everyone helped. In addition, one took events like games. The last two planned booths and decorations. The list of suggestions for names of the town grew until finally someone suggested Hope. No one added anymore after that and people started calling the town Hope. The vote for the name Friday before the fair opened was no surprise. Saturday afternoon was clear and sunny. As the people walked into town, they saw a large platform had been set up for the speeches. There were several chairs on it and guessing who would get to sit in them was a favorite pastime. There were five booths. One held small carved figures that Bert had made to sell. One was collection of hand sewn pieces including aprons, potholders and small toys. These had been donated by the women of town to help cover the costs for the fair. Another had a large container of lemonade. The fourth one was a game with bottles and rings and the

149

last held plants and seeds. Gerald was running that booth. Just outside of town a field had been set up for a race and an area was set aside for picnics. There were tables of food set up with each family contributing something. Sam and Anne had provided the main course, but everyone brought side dishes that showed their skills as a cook. There were amazing desserts available in case anyone was hungry after all that food. Yet another table held pitchers of water and a few pots of coffee. Someone had started a campfire with a grate over it to keep the coffee boiling. Every household had been told to bring their own place settings if they wanted to eat. In the fields around the house there was an area set up for races, picnics, the goats milled around inside a hastily built enclosure and puppies peeped out of a large box. It was controlled chaos, and everyone was delighted. It had been decided that the speeches would start at eleven o clock and they were warned to be done by noon so people could eat. Sam mounted the steps to the platform and called the mine manager and each of the shaft managers up with him. He then called up the four women who had planned the event. When each of them was seated He began by praising and thanking the women who had planned the event. He gave each of them a plaque handmade by Bert stating that they were the first to plan "Naming Day" in the town of

Hope. He then Unveiled a sign which stated, "Welcome to Hope" It was to be placed beside the road telling everyone that they were a real town. He suggested that the store owners consider renaming their buildings appropriately. He asked each shaft manager to come forward and showed them a large piece of wood with their names, the date and shaft numbers on it. Across the top it said, "Hope Mining Company Shaft Supervisors" He praised each of their efforts and announced how much coal had come out of each shaft in the last 6 months. His mine manager was called up and praised as well. He received a small name plate for his desk. Sam talked about each booth and assured everyone jokingly that he wouldn't see a penny from any of them. He also announced that the plant booth had flower plants and seeds as well as vegetable seeds available. Each family would be able to receive a packet of seeds for the garden next year if they wanted and each woman could get either a packet of seeds or a plant to put around their house. He joked that Gerald's garden was looking rather sparse, so he hoped everyone thanked him for his work. He then announced the schedule of events and invited everyone to eat. He cautioned them to save him chocolate cake and everyone laughed. At exactly noon he cut a ceremonial ribbon opening the fair. About half the people surged towards the food. Several of the men headed for the dessert table first and then carried around a piece of chocolate cake making sure Sam saw them enjoying it. Playing along Sam frowned each time he saw someone with "his" cake but when he saw Shawn taking part in the joke gleefully, he raced after him trying to get a bite. The children were shrieking in delight when they saw this and clamored for dessert first as well. Laughing the woman herded their husbands and little ones to the picnic area for some healthy food first. The booths were doing a great deal of business as well. Many women now held a packet of seeds and a few a hardy plant. The men were enjoying an argument over what should be planted by which of them. Teens were trying desperately to get a ring around a soda bottle thus winning a coveted cola drink. Children begged for a carved or fabric toy and several women proudly gave money for an apron or a potholder. Spare money for a toy or pretty apron would have been unheard of 6 months ago but now almost every child had a penny or two to spend. Prices were kept low this first year. Bert sold most of his pieces for one or two cents. The lemonade was a penny a ladle, but you needed your own cup. The ring toss was a penny as well. Aprons went for five cents and toys for two or three. All the money went towards expenses for next year's fair. A cheer went up the first time a youngster managed to toss the ring over a bottle and he proudly held up his bottle. It was the first time any of them had tasted the drink. His success created a new surge of kids anxious to try their luck.   Each of the King children except for James had received a penny as well. The girls bought toys, but Shawn bought his mother a potholder. It had flowers on it like the sugar bag in the house kitchen, so he was sure she'd like it. Sam asked him why he had done that, and he said. "Daddy isn't here to give her a wildflower bouquet for her birthday like he always used to, so I thought I'd get her something with flowers on it. " With tears in his eyes Sam hugged the boy and whispered that he was proud of him. He then asked when the big day was, and assured him, he would see that it was celebrated royally. Shawn asked him to tuck the present into his pocket, so his mother didn't see it and Sam did. He suggested to Fiona when he saw her herding her charges to the picnic blanket set out for them that the girls color pictures of flowers for Anne and that even James be allowed a crayon and a piece of paper to make the event more memorable. With that he went in search of his wife who was helping to organize the three-legged race. Unbeknownst to the townspeople Sam had put up a prize for each of the races. First place was $1.00. Second place .50 and third .25. Everyone was thrilled. There was a sack race, a three-legged race and a foot race with a twist. Each contestant had to carry a full glass of water and whoever got to the finish line with the most water won regardless of how fast he was. Everyone laughed when the water started spilling. One enterprising young man walked to the finish line. He was last in, but his water cup barely spilled a drop. He accepted his dollar proudly. After all the races everyone settled in to watch the promised demonstration of Bella's abilities. First Adam scattered the goats all over the field then much to everyone's surprise he sat down, and Shawn got up. The nine-year-old went to the center of the field and whistled. In seconds Bella came running up to him and sat at his feet. He raised his arm waved it in a circle and pointed to a corner of the field. Bella launched into action. Within the space of five minutes she had the goats congregated in the corner he had pointed to and was back at his feet eager for another task. Shawn looked at Adam who nodded. "Take em home girl." Shawn yelled and Bella dove for the goats. Everyone watched open mouthed as she drove them towards the stable in the Kings yard. Adam stood up then and talked about different things the dogs could be taught to do. He offered to teach anyone who wanted a dog how to train it. He finished by calling Shawn back to show everyone Titan's progress. By then every child in the audience over age three was begging for a puppy. Adam had no problem finding good homes for Bella's last few or even the ones found in the den. The field then became a baseball field. The women watched over sleeping toddlers and babies while the men and older boys played ball. One of the women organized a game for those too old to nap but too young to play with the men in another part of the field. Some people visited the food tables again. When the baseball game ended everyone laughed to see Sam following Jennifer out onto the field. She was carrying one of her chocolate cakes swirled with icing. She presented it to the winning team to share and Sam pretended to be sad. When he got to the edge of the field a shout went up as the women who were standing there moved to one side revealing Anne holding another chocolate cake. She presented it to him, and everyone cheered when he hugged her and placed a light kiss on her lips. After all the games were over and the booths sold out people packed up their children and belongings for the trip home. The party had been a success and several women were heard planning next year's event. The money from the donated items yielded a start to expenses for it. The problem was no one could decide who should take charge of the money in the meantime. They finally brought the money to Sam and asked him to hold onto it. Sam decided that the town needed a bank.

Chapter 9

More Challenges

Things were settling down and preparation for the fourth of July were under way when Sam got a letter that his mother was missing. The first thing he did was hire Bert as guard again, explaining that if she showed up, he was to detain her and under no circumstances let her near Anne or the children. He told Anne what was going on and brought Adam and Gerald in on the news as well. Anne insisted on praying for her and sent pictures the children had colored with him. Then he left for Tennessee. When he arrived, he found that she had slipped away in the night. Her guards had the flu and had fallen asleep one night. They had already searched the town and surrounding countryside. She was nowhere to be found. Sam talked to the man running the ticket window at the train station and he said that no one fitting her description had bought a ticket in the last two weeks. Sam went to the conductor of the train he had come in on and asked about someone fitting her description. The conductor remembered her. She had entered a first-class compartment and taken it over. When he came by for her ticket, she acted like she owned the railroad. "It was amazing," He said. "She had me convinced she was almost royalty.

Then I realized she didn't have any luggage and that seemed strange. I talked it over with the engineer and we decided to take her to the authorities and let them handle it. So, we turned her over to the sheriff in the next town and left. You know her? Was she important and all?" Sam asked him to notify him immediately if he ever saw her again and bought a ticket for the town his mother was in. He sent a note to the house he'd rented for her to tell the guards to have everything packed up, close the house and follow him. When he got to the sheriff's office, he could hear his mother demanding to be let out. The sheriff looked up when he entered. "Yes? Sorry about the noise, one of our guests doesn't like the accommodations." Sam grimaced. "I can hear that. What will it cost me to get her out of jail? She escaped from her companions and I need to get her back where she won't hurt anyone. " The sheriff nodded. "I was wondering if she escaped from a ...well a locked facility. Her thirty days are half over so if you pay the cost of the ticket and what she's cost me staying here, you can have her. Honestly though having her here has cut down on crime in my little town. No one wants to be in jail with her. Even the drunks have sobered up for a spell." Sam smiled wryly and paid the fine and fees. Following the sheriff back he faced his mother. "Well." He said, "Not your best idea mother is it?" "Sam," she yelled.

"Get me out of here. I'll even go back to that awful house. At least there the bedding was softer." Holding herself regally she swept from the cell. Glaring at the sheriff she haughtily said. "I will not be giving you a positive recommendation sir; in fact, I will do my best to have you shut down. I can see why I was your only guest. And fix that door! it sticks horribly." "Yes Ma'am." The sheriff muttered. Sam shook his head and ushered his mother out of the jail and down to the train station. By the time the train arrived his mother had run through all the complaints about the house, the train conductor, the sheriff, the courtroom and the anything else she could think of, twice. When her guards got off the train she stood up and declared. "No, I am not going back to that house. I won't spend another minute there. These people don't listen to me." "No mother, they don't listen to you. I pay them to listen to me. And no, you don't have to go back to that house. Remember I told you if you caused any trouble you would go to a more remote place with less comforts. This is your last chance. If you make trouble or escape again, I will put you in an institution. I'm trying to be patient mother, but you could have been hurt or sent to prison. You'll stay in a hotel here until I make arrangements for another home. If you make too much noise the hotel will complain, and they will have to put you back in jail. You must stay in the room. If you are behaving, you may go to the dining room for dinner otherwise your guards will bring you a plate when they eat. I love you and want you to be comfortable but more than that I want you safe." After promising the guards he'd be in touch he took the next train out. Stopping off at the town before his he stopped at his attorney's office to make sure his will was up to date and then went to the bank to find out how to get a branch started in Hope. After finding out that the bank had a policy against putting branches in towns without a police force, he then went to the sheriff to see how to accomplish that. When he got home, he sent Adam to post notices about a town meeting the next night. When he walked into the house it was silent. It was as quiet as it would be at 3 A.M. Running up the stairs to the nursery he found it empty, no toys out of place, beds made but no one there. Anne's room was the same. Fear rising inside he quickly took the servants stairs to the kitchen.   When he got there, he saw Jennifer dozing at the table with a cup of tea cooling in front of her. When he came bursting in, she jumped up spilling her tea. "Oh Sir!" she exclaimed. "You scared me. Is something wrong?" "My family, where are they?" Sam asked as calmly as he could. "Oh, they and most of the staff went down to the town to help clean the church. The new minister is arriving tomorrow, and we can have church again. Did you need something Sir? You look a bit pale. Sit down, I'll get you some milk and cookies. My cookies always make you feel better." Sam sat down in relief. He ate a few cookies being careful to compliment her and drank the milk. When he heard the front door he rose, thanked Cook and went to meet his family. They were almost as happy to see him as he was to see them. He hugged Anne first and gently kissed her cheek loving how it made her blush. Then he turned to the children clamoring for their turn. Seeing tears in Amy's eyes he picked her up and asked, "What is making my little one sad today?" Amy held up her finger. "I got a splinter and it hurt a lot when Mommy took it out." "Ah" Sam nodded. " I was just told the best cure for making someone feel better." "What is it?" Asked Amy warily. "I don't want any yucky medicine." "Even if it will make you feel better?" Asked Sam. "I know the best splinter medicine of all. In fact, I just had some. "Did you get a sp'inter too?" asked April. "No, my sweet, this medicine cures a whole lot of things. Now you all go tell Miss Jennifer that you need some medicine just like Papa and show her your splinter." directed Sam. "But we didn't get splinters. " explained Shawn. "Just Amy." "Well, you can always refuse the medicine when you get there, or you can take it to celebrate that you didn't get a splinter. It's up to you." chuckled Sam. The children ran off in the direction of the kitchen and Sam put his arm around Anne. "I want to hear all about your day darling and I have a few things to run past you as well." Smiling Anne took his hand and they walked to the library. This time Sam sat in a chair next to her still holding her hand. While she told him how everyone was and what activities the kids had been up to, he listened intently. He then told her about his adventures. He glossed over the problems with his mother, just telling her that he had located her, and she was all right. He discussed having a police force come in and a bank set up in town and asked her to come to the meeting tomorrow night. When he was done, Anne brought the subject of his mother back up. She insisted on knowing what exactly happened. Sam reluctantly explained and Anne suggested she be brought home. Sam refused to allow her near his family for fear she would cause problems. After a bit of discussion, they reached a compromise. On the east side of the house overlooking the flower garden was an unused wing. They would prepare rooms for Abigail and her companions to live there. Sam insisted that the connecting door be boarded up in case she had stashed keys somewhere and would have a new door from the outside They would bring her to the house when the children were sleeping so they didn't realize she was there. Anne promised to talk to the little ones and calm their fears of being around her. Anne was hoping that Sam's mother would want to be a grandmother if she saw the children, but she didn't mention that to Sam. She suggested they schedule a weekly meeting with the new minister instead of requiring church on Sunday which Sam agreed was a great idea. Soon the children came in excited from their mid-day treat. Fiona followed but Anne waved her away. They spent some family time in the library reading books and acting out parts for an hour until James ended it all by crawling over to Sam's lap and pulling himself upright by bracing himself on Sam's shoulder. He looked at Anne and said "Mammmma." Then he looked at Sam and said, "Papapapa" Everyone clapped excitedly, and the startled baby let go and dropped back on his bottom which only made the other children laugh harder. James couldn't decide if he should cry or laugh at first but then joined in the merriment. Sam was dancing around yelling "He said my name!"

Scooping him up Anne declared it time to wash up for supper. "I hope everyone is still hungry." She said looking pointedly at Sam. Sam just winked at her. At the meeting the next night Sam explained that in order to have a bank, they must first have a police force or some sort of law enforcement coverage. He went on to say that he had talked his

162

lawyer into sending someone to town twice a month to take care of any business that might need to be done. He then asked if anyone had anything to say. Caleb stood. "I think we need some sort of government. We should have some sort of police force in case something happens. I don't think Mr. King should be the one to pay for it though. It's our town. We need to do somethings for ourselves. Now that we get a decent wage, we can afford to pay something each to cover the costs. We should consider some fire equipment as well. It would be a volunteer company, but we'd need to buy equipment. Everyone started murmuring and Sam motioned Caleb forward. When he reached the front. Sam put a hand on his shoulder and turned to the crowd. "I nominate Caleb to be the new mayor of Hope, Pennsylvania." The men roared agreement and the women clapped. "Then it's settled." Sam asked? "No one disagrees?" Caleb looked a bit dazed when Sam shook his hand and walked to the back of the room. "Just before he left, he whispered, "The meeting is all yours now." Shaking his head Caleb faced the crowd. "OK we need a committee to decide what to do first. I suggest each shaft pick someone from each shift to be their representative. We need someone from the town businesses as well. That makes a committee of six, five men and me. We'll .." Three women rose and interrupted him all speaking at once. Caleb held up his hand for order. "Wait. We can't understand you when you all speak at once." The women looked at each other and came to some sort of silent agreement on who would be spokesperson. "We feel that their needs to be equal representation on that committee. The United States may not have given us the right to vote yet but it's headed that way and we don't feel it is fair for men to make all the decisions." The room was in an uproar at that point. Caleb called for order. "I'm sorry ladies, I apologize. It is only fair that we have a woman or two on the committee as well. Everyone in town should have an equal say. We need a real election. I'll ask Cecil to put up a list in his window so anyone who wants to can run for one of the positions. We'll keep it to six or we'll never get past the talking stage. Then next week we'll have our election. Does that sit well with everyone?" From the back one of the men spoke up. "I don't want no woman deciding how much I can afford to pay for stuff in town. They don't understand enough to make decisions."   At that his wife stood up and stalked back to him. "Leroy" she hissed. "You are full of it. I've been doing our finances for years. Most of the rest of these women do as well. You better get used to the idea of women having an equal say in things. Hope isn't just a men's town you know." Leroy blustered. "Yeah, what are you gonna do? Leave me?" "Yes" countered his wife. "You forget I can get a job now. I don't have to be dependent on you to feed me and put a roof over my head. So, either you start treating me as an equal or I leave." Turning to the other men who were watching this exchange she added. "We all will. We have options now." The men all looked at their wives who were grimly nodding their heads. One of the men raised his hand and when Caleb nodded at him, he said. "Women on the committee is fine with me. We wouldn't have survived the last few years since old Mr. King died if they hadn't been able to stretch a penny till it squealed." The other men nodded, and Caleb dismissed the meeting reminding them to all check the store window and then vote next week. Sam and Anne walked home arm in arm talking quietly about how Hope was growing. The vote was taken, and the committee ended up with 4 men and 2 women. The first thing they did was start the process of becoming incorporated. They sent for bylaws from several town and took what they felt would fit their town from them and put that to a vote. The town next to them had their own newspaper and they sent someone to talk to the editor about starting a branch in Hope. They agreed that the paper would have a page dedicated to news in Hope for now and if enough people subscribed would consider branching out after a year. A reporter was appointed to come to

Hope every week to see what news there was and to sell advertisements. The next stop they made in that town was to the sheriff's office. One of the deputies who was about to retire was willing to come to Hope but they weren't sure what to do about a salary.   He suggested that providing a house for he and his wife would cut down the cost of what they had to pay him. He also said it sounded like they only needed him part time, at least for now. He was even willing to use his own vehicle if they paid for gas and maintained the car. Cars were becoming more possible to the people who lived in Hope and they had been approached by a young man who wanted to open a garage there. When the committee met again, they discussed options for raising the money to pay the salary for the deputy. They also talked about the need for fire equipment in town. The committee invited Sam to come in and asked his advice for raising money. Sam suggested that they start with a very low tax to pay the police department and to start to build a surplus. He told them he would donate housing space for the officer and his wife to stay in, but agreed that the town had to start paying its own way. He also suggested they advertise for men who were interested in starting a volunteer fire company. Someone would have to go door to door and sell its service to pay for the equipment but he was willing to provide space for storing that equipment and allow mine workers to leave without worrying about being fired when the whistle blew if they had registered as a member of the department with their supervisor. He wasn't going to pay them for the time spent away from the job, but he will allow them to count the hours against vacation if they choose. He couldn't speak for the other businesses in town though. The mine was no longer the only place of employment in town, there were several businesses moving into the buildings on Main Street. Besides the Grocers, Sundries Shop, and Produce Market there was the Doctor's office, an Attorney's office, although he was only there once a week, and an office the newspaper man used once a week. Sam had had the men build several other buildings and a large warehouse while they waited for the safety equipment to arrive. He picked one of them to be the sheriff's office with rooms for them to stay in above. The warehouse was being used to store equipment and contents that no one needed from the old houses. He had it cleaned out and partitioned off half the space for the fire department. The last building, he had still was a large one with several rooms. He was hoping it would become the Hope Hotel someday. As each store or business started up, he sold the building to the person starting it, at a major discount. While it meant he ran the risk of someone coming in and buying everything he felt owning all the buildings in town made him a dictator. There was one building in town that he had never owned. His mother had given the land to a cousin for some reason who promptly sold it. The owner ran the local saloon. It was two doors down from the soon to be sheriff's office. The saloon's owner had tried to buy the hotel from him, but Sam was afraid it wouldn't become quite the hotel he had envisioned and refused. The town was growing. The committee decided that they would tax the stores a certain amount each year as well as the townspeople. They kept it as low as they could, but they knew some people would object. It was hard to decide how to tax people. Should they tax someone who had a better job and made more money more than others? That would mean they had to have access to salary amounts. No one wanted to tell how much they made. If they taxed everyone the same that wasn't fair either. A woman doing laundry to feed her family shouldn't have to pay the same as a shaft supervisor. They finally decided to have the businesses see to collecting taxes for each employee. It made more paperwork for the business but less of a headache for the committee. They also discussed the schoolteacher. The state had been paying him, but they should really take that on as a town. All of this brought back the question of a bank of their own. Now that they had a police force, they could make arrangements for the bank to start a branch there in town. They decided to ask Sam to sell the building that the attorney and newspaper man used to the bank and have them rent office space in another building. Cecil who had started attending meetings as an observer when he realized they were going to start taxing him volunteered to rent an office out of his building that the attorney and newspaper man could share as long as they came on separate days. He had added it on so that he could have a post office there, but the Sundries store had beaten him to it and arranged to have the post office branch at his place. Every time they figured out how to deal with some aspect of being a town, something new came up for them to deal with. It was challenging and frustrating, but they stuck with it determined to see Hope become a thriving town someday.

Chapter 10

Abigail

Abigail and her entourage arrived about two week later. The children were still scared of her but understood that she was Sam's mother and needed a safe place to stay. They were asleep when she arrived. Anne insisted on being there to welcome her. Abigail looked at her but didn't say anything. She followed Sam around the rooms they had set up for her and her companions and then went to bed. The next morning breakfast was served in front of the window overlooking the garden. Abigail sat staring out at the flowers. She could see Gerald in the distance doing something with the roses. She spent the next several days quietly thinking usually in front of the garden. When she had been there a week, she sent a note to Sam asking that Anne stop to visit. Sam talked with Anne about it. He didn't want her to go but Anne insisted that they give her a chance. The companions say she has been quite docile and even cooperative. They'll be there and you can insist one stay in the room if you like. Reluctantly Sam agreed to let her go for an hour. He insisted on waiting outside the door the whole time and told her to call out if she needed him. Anne kissed him and wrote a note back accepting the invitation. The next day she knocked on the door and was admitted. Sam put a chair by the entrance and sat down. He refused to have the door closed. Anne was shown into the room Abigail used for a parlor where tea and cookies were waiting. Abigail entered a few minutes later. Anne turned to her and smiled. "Thank you for inviting me." Abigail's sharp eyes took in her slim build. "Well, you dress better than you used to." she sniffed. Anne smiled at her. "Yes, dressing well is much easier now. Would you like a new dress Abigail? I'm sure Sam would be glad to have one made. The seamstress in town is very talented." "Seamstress in town" said Abigail sharply. "Sam's going to lose everything if he keeps paying for stuff like that. This town didn't need a seamstress when his father was alive, and it doesn't need one now. What else is he wasting money on?" Anne explained that the seamstress wasn't paid by them. She is independent. In fact, she bought her store from us and had hired a couple women to help in her shop. One of them is an excellent milliner. When was the last time you had a new hat? Perhaps we could go shopping together sometime and find you a nice outfit." "Something wrong with the one I have on missy?" spate her mother in law. Anne heard Sam start in the door and quickly answered gently. "Of course not. It is lovely I just thought it

171

might be fun to go shopping. Sam told me you used to love hats. If you speak loudly Sam might not let me come back and I'd like to visit with you every week." Abigail looked at her. "Why? I'm mean to you and your children are afraid of me. What do you want to come here for?" Anne stood "I want to come because you are Sam's mother and the grandmother of our children. They have a lot of love to give and I think you would enjoy them in small doses." As she finished speaking Sam came to the door. "Time to go my darling." Abigail looked at him and whispered. "Bring her back next week at the same time." And left the room. Before next week came Anne had paid a visit to the seamstress and bought a dark grey poplin and a hat to match. She also had several patterns for her mother in law to choose from. Armed with this and a few colored pictures the children had made she knocked on the door. Sam again sat in a chair waiting. This time Abigail was waiting in the parlor. "I didn't have them make tea since you didn't drink any last time and I ate the last cookie a few minutes ago." She snapped. "That's fine" said Anne "I wouldn't want to get anything on the fabric I brought anyway. What do you think of it?" Abigail fingered the piece of material. "Well at least you know how to pick a good fabric." She admitted. "What's in that box?" She pointed at the hat box. Anne handed it to her to open. After removing tissues from the top, she held up a hat. It was beautiful, just the kind she used to love when her husband was alive.   It was so tempting to put it on and turn to the mirror. Resisting she put it back into the box and closed the lid. "Don't have anywhere to wear a hat like that or a dress made from that stuff. If you want me to get measured though I guess I will. Better than having Sam spend all the money on hiring people for the town." Anne solemnly sat down beside her and showed her the patterns. "Which one would you prefer, or which do you dislike least?" she asked. Abigail glanced at her, but Anne wasn't smiling so she looked at the patterns. "I guess this one will do. Still don't know where I can wear it though. Nothing in this town to do. I don't know about the color. I've worn black ever since my husband died. Maybe it'll be ok. Have her trim it in black." Anne nodded and then Sam was there to help her pick up the packages and after promising to come back in a week they left. On the tea table were the pictures the children had colored for her. Each one said, "To Grandmother" and was signed. The next week Anne came back bearing a large box. Abigail's eyes sparkled when she looked at it until she realized that Anne was smiling and then she looked away quickly. Anne opened the box and pulled out a beautiful grey dress with black trim that matched the hat she had brought last week perfectly. "I suppose you want me to try that thing on?" Abigail asked. "No, that's ok you don't have to" replied Anne laying the dress across a chair. When you do though, you might try on both, so we know if they fit." Replied Anne quietly. "Other one? You wasted more of my son's money on another dress? Why do I need more than one and I didn't even need that!" huffed her mother in law. "Very well then I won't pull it out. It goes with this hat by the way." Anne pulled out a beautiful medium blue hat perfect for Abigail's white curls. Abigail couldn't contain her small gasp of delight but then she covered with a cough. "Oh my, I hope you aren't coming down with something." Commented Anne. "Perhaps I'd better go so you can get some rest. Next week I'll bring some chocolate cake that we're having for Shawn's birthday and you can tell me if the dresses fit." Anne left before her mother in law could say another word. Abigail went to the box and pulled the other dress from the tissue paper. It was a beautiful blue with a darker blue trim. Just the kind of thing she would have chosen if she had let herself pick something pretty these past few years. Hugging the dress and picking up the matching hat she went to her bedroom. Her companion brought the grey dress and hat to her, placed them on a chair and left the room. Abigail changed into the blue dress and then risked a peek in the mirror. She stood

174

staring at someone she hadn't seen in many years. Stumbling to a chair she sat down, overcome with the memories of things she had done over the years that her husband would never have approved of. He had been frugal, but she had become mean. When had she become someone so greedy that people were afraid of her? Children used to bring joy and now they were afraid of her and called her a witch. She had once encouraged Sam to study his Bible but then one night she took it away and put it on the highest shelf in the library. Then she sent him away from her to boarding schools. She kept him away from his best friend and even hired people to spy on him. She thought back to her escape from the house he'd placed her in and realized the memories were fuzzy of that time. The change in environment seemed to have brought on a pea soup thick fog that she had had trouble navigating. It was like what her mother described just before she died. She seemed alright most of the time but occasionally she would wander off and have to be brought home. She was never sure where she was or why she had left until that last time when they found her body in the river. The church investigated very thoroughly before agreeing to let her be buried in the churchyard. That was the last time she went to church or spoke to a minister before Sam started having one brought to the house every week. Abigail fell to her knees and begged to be left aware of who she was and where she was until the end. While she was on them, she discussed a few more of her failings that she had discovered. The blue dress was like magic. Rising she felt renewed and alive again. Taking off the dress and putting on the grey one she rang for her companion and requested dinner in the parlor. She invited the two who were constantly with her to join her instead of eating in their room as usual. She called them by name, Heather and Karen, for the very first time. Startled by the changes they sat with her. Abigail asked about their families and thanked them for taking such good care of her. When dinner was over, she said good night and wished them pleasant dreams for the first time since they'd started living with her. Heather, who usually worked the night shift decided to write a report to Sam about what had happened. The next morning Abigail told them she like them to eat with her all the time from now on when their duties permitted. She was again wearing the grey dress. The blue one was hanging in the closet. Karen found a note addressed to Anne, and one for Sam on the side table and put them with the one Heather had written. When someone came to remove the breakfast dishes, she asked him to give the notes to Sam. Sam found the notes on the desk when he went to the library after reading to the children. Recognizing his mother's handwriting he braced himself for what she might say. His jaw dropped when he read it.

My dear son,

I'm so very sorry for the way I've been treating you since we lost your father. Actually, since Grandmama died. Your Bible is on the top shelf in the library behind the set of Shakespeare your grandfather used to read. You didn't lose it, I stole it and I am very sorry. I suspect you have another one by now, but you might enjoy seeing your old one again. I am also sorry for sending you away. I am glad it didn't ruin your friendship with Donald. You were right to take over the mine. I was behaving abysmally, and I only hope you can forgive me and make amends on my behalf.

Now as to your new family. I've only met your wife, but I am praying that can be remedied soon. I want to be Grandmama to those four precious little ones you've made my family. Anne is beautiful, gracious,

178

and generous. All things I have not been for quite some time. I wrote a note to your wife asking for her forgiveness and for chance to be Grandmama to her little ones. I hope you will give it to her. I love you son. Your wife opened my eyes to what I had become, and I will spend the rest of my days trying to make up for it.

Love,

Mother

P.S Please send me a Sears catalog.

The note for Anne held an apology and an invitation to bring any of the children that were willing to meet her with her the next week.

Sam fell to his knees in thanksgiving and Anne found him there when she came from tucking the children in bed. Fearing the worst when she saw him sobbing she put her arms around him and held him. When he recovered enough to speak he hugged her and told her how awesome she was. Confused she looked at him and then saw the letters he was holding. Taking the one addressed to her she began to read. Sam started looking through the books on the top shelf. Finding Shakespeare, he moved several volumes and found his childhood Bible, given to him by his Grandmama. Turning he found Anne staring at him tears in her eyes. They sat on the chairs Sam had placed side by side, holding hands and praising God for the miracle that had come to them. Then they started going thru the Bible looking at his childish notes and seeing what passages had been important to him at that young age. The inscription in the front read. "To my first grandson, Samuel Jason King. From his Grandmama, because I love him." Smiling Anne said. "Now I know why you wrote that in Shawn's Bible. What a wonderful tradition. She laid her head on his shoulder. Before Sam went to bed that night, he wrote a note to his mother thanking her and telling her he loved her. He tucked it into the Sears catalog and took them down to the kitchen so Jennifer could have them delivered with breakfast. He never even read the note from her companions until the next morning. The report made him even happier. Whistling he went to work. Anne pulled Shawn aside after school and explained that Sam's mother wanted to meet him. He agreed immediately which surprised her. He said they should keep it secret from the girls since they were afraid of her still and Anne agreed. The next week She, Shawn and James went for the visit. Grandmama was waiting for them in the blue dress. Shawn solemnly shook her hand and James waved from the safety of Anne's arms. As promised, Anne had brought chocolate cake and milk. After everyone had enjoyed their treat and James was cleaned up, he climbed down from his mother's lap and started to explore the room a bit. Shawn was playing in the corner with a couple of tin soldiers he had found in the nursery. Abigail watched the little ones with a smile on her face. Suddenly she sat up sharply. "Shawn." She called "What do you have there?" Shawn looked up at Anne who nodded and then crossed the room to his grandmother. "They're soldier figures. I found them in a box in the nursery." Shawn handed the figures to her. Grandmama examined them and handed them back. "I remember buying these for my son's Christmas stocking many years ago. I'm glad you're enjoying them." Shawn smiled at her. "I knew coming to see you would be ok. I figured anyone who raised my Papa couldn't be scary all the time." Anne started when he used to word "scary," but Abigail waved her back. "I'm sorry I was scary. If I ever get like that again, please tell me so I can stop." "I will Grandmama. I promise" answered Shawn. James had managed to get across the room and was pulling on Abigail's skirts. Reaching down she picked him up and settled him on her lap where he proceeded to play with and chew on the buttons decorating her dress. Smiling Grandmama reached out a hand and pulled Shawn in for a hug as well. She whispered something Anne couldn't hear, and Shawn nodded vigorously. Shortly afterwards they left so Shawn could get his chores done before dinner. When Sam got home, he went straight to the nursery to ask about the visit. The report gave him hope. When he got to the library, he found the Sears Catalog on his desk with a list in it. The list included a toy suitable for each grandchild and a couple of everyday dresses. There was also a request for a couple of pieces of her jewelry to be returned. Sam sent the list to town and then went to the safe to get the jewelry. He decided to deliver it himself. When he was ushered into his mother's parlor, he found her reading her Bible. Looking up she came to him with a smile and hugged him for the first time he could remember since he was 10 years old. Gratefully he hugged her back and then seated her again. Sitting in the chair opposite he placed the jewelry pieces on the table before her. She picked them up and said, "Which of these do you think Anne would like?" I was thinking the Ruby but if you think she'd like the Emerald better I could give her that." Sam stared for a second. "You wanted to see these to give one to Anne?" "Why yes" she replied they were given to me when I joined the family, it seems only right that she gets them now. Actually, I'd like to give her only one. The other two are for Amy and April when they grow up. Is that ok or do you need the money they could bring in?" Sam beamed at her. "That's just fine Mother, Anne will be pleased to have anything you choose to give her." "I'm saving the other pieces in case the two of you have more girls later. You'll keep them safe for me, won't you? That reminds me did you approve my Sear's list?" "Yes, but I'm not sure why you wanted the four lengths of fabric and some ready-made dresses." "Well, the fabric is for Heather and Karen. If we're to be spending time as a family, then they have to wear prettier clothes than those uniforms you issued them.

183

Goodness they're all black. That could scare a child. I want them to wear pretty dresses when my grandchildren are around. The ready mades are for me. I love the dresses Anne had made for me but holding and playing with children can be very hard on clothes. James was chewing on the buttons of my favorite blue dress just yesterday. He didn't ruin anything, and I wouldn't really care if he did, but it seemed prudent to have a few casual dresses for playing with my grandchildren." Sam grinned. "That's fine mother, we can burn those black things and put everyone in flowered uniforms if you want!" His mother laughed at him and sent him off to dinner. The next week Anne brought the girls with her to visit. They were reluctant but obedient. When they got there Grandmother was in a rose-colored dress with tiny white flowers on it. She had a couple packages next to her. The children sat at their mother's feet, April holding part of her mother's dress in front of her face. Grandmama talked with Anne for a bit and then asked the children to tell her about their kittens. As they talked about the havoc the two little creatures wreaked in the nursery every day the girls became more animated and the hand holding her mother's dress was used to gesture instead of hide. They told her about the pony as well and Grandmother told them about Sam's pony. His name was Bouncy. The girls laughed when she said that. After a bit she asked what the girls liked to do. Slowly but surely she brought them out of their shell by asking questions and paying attention to the answers.   Just before the time was up, she asked if they would like a present since she had missed their birthday. The girls nodded vigorously, and Abigail held out the gaily wrapped packages. Cautiously they approached her to claim them. Seeing two more on the table Amy asked. "Are the other two for our brothers?" "Yes," replied Grandmother "since I missed their birthdays as well. Will you deliver them for me?" Nodding the two little girls took the packages and sat on the floor to open them. Grandmother smiled when they sat at her feet instead of returning to their mother. Inside each package was a skipping rope. Delighted the girls ran to show their mother who raised an eyebrow at them. Getting the message, the girls walked over to grandmother and politely thanked her. April leaned on her knee and asked what was in the boys' packages. "I got Shawn some marbles and James a jack in the box." she replied. "Do you think they'll like them?" "Oh yes" said Amy, "they'll love them. You pick out great gifts Grandmama." Smiling Abigail gently placed a hand on each girl's back. "I'm glad you think so she whispered." April looked into her eyes. "Grandmama when you smile, you're not a scary. Can you smile more?" Anne opened her mouth but Grandmama spoke first. "What a good idea sweetheart. I'll try that. Perhaps you girls can remind me when I forget. After all, I'm out of practice." Nodding the girls took their mother's hand and they left carrying the boys presents. so the girls could get chores done before supper.

The next day there was a note inviting Sam and Anne to come to tea alone. When they arrived, they found both companions and Abigail waiting for them. After everyone had one of Jennifer's excellent sugar cookies and a cup of tea in hand Abigail began explaining that she wanted to be a part of their lives. She asked if she could come to church with them and perhaps be included in family celebrations. She then told them that she wanted the companions to continue and the doors between her wing and the rest of the house to stay locked. Frowning Sam asked why. Abigail explained about what her mother was like the last few years of her life. Anne went to her and hugged her and promised that they would protect her from that happening to her. Hugging her back Abigail told her that having the children around would give her a longer life for sure. The companions agreed to watch carefully and keep the keys. Another set would be made for Anne so that the children could visit without her having to borrow Sam's set. Regular visits were set up with the children and they invited her to join them at lunch from time to time if she could stand the chaos. Family life was improving at the King house.

Chapter 11

Something to Celebrate

The children and Anne were getting used to their new way of life. It was a relief to not have to worry about if there would be a next meal or if Shawn would have to drop out of school and go to the rock pile. The children were expected to do chores still, but they had more energy and could enjoy their free time more because of that. Anne and Sam didn't want to spoil them. Well, actually Sam did want to spoil them, but bowed to Anne's more experienced opinion. When birthdays came around though they both worked hard to make sure the child felt special. There was always a lavish cake and gifts. Each birthday boy or girl received three gifts just like the Christ child had received when the wise men came. Anne insisted one of the gifts be practical and Sam wanted one to be readable. The other was something they wanted. The kids never caught on to why the Sears catalog turned up in the nursery a month or so before each child's birthday and then couldn't be found just before. At least if they caught on, they never let the adults know they knew. If school was in session on the birthday, they were allowed to take Cook's special cookies to share with their classmates. Anne refused to hold birthday parties because that placed an added burden on their friend's parents who couldn't afford to have one for their children or send a gift. Sam celebrated Anne's birthday in much the same way although he never had to resort to leaving the Sears catalog around. Anne didn't do much that first year for Sam's birthday because it occurred only a month after their wedding. The next year however she was determined to make up for it. Sam had been ever so patient with her and allowed her time to grieve the loss of Donald. He grieved with her and many times they sat in the library talking about him. Lately she realized that they laughed together at his antics more than they cried together over the loss. She also realized that slowly but surely, she had fallen in love with Sam over the months. She knew Sam loved her and she decided that for his birthday they would remarry. That would give them an anniversary to celebrate that wasn't three days after the death of her first love and the children's father. She decided not to tell Sam of the plans. She took the cook into her confidence and Jennifer was busy for days making a beautiful wedding cake. The minister and his family had been in town for several months and was quite popular. She asked him to request a meeting with Sam keep him occupied so they could decorate. When Sam got the note asking him to come to the church to discuss an issue of great importance, he told Anne who suggested he bring the Reverend and his wife home for dinner afterwards. Agreeing to do just that Sam set off. He was feeling a bit down since no one had mentioned his birthday and he figured if there was company for dinner then it had been forgotten. Shrugging he decided it didn't really matter. The meeting confused him because it didn't seem like anything important was brought up. He extended and had accepted the dinner invitation when he first got there so after three hours of a report on the church finances and a discussion of the importance of revivals the three of them started for the house. Sam had brought the carriage so that he could take them all. When they got there Fiona opened the door. Sam asked where Anne was, and she replied that she'd be right there. She then said that the children were in the library waiting for him. On the door of the library was a sign obviously made by Amy that said, "Happy Birthday Papa" Delighted Sam opened the door to see what the children had planned for him. He was stunned when he saw them sitting quietly in dressy clothes and standing at the front was his beautiful wife wearing a lacy dress holding a bouquet of flowers. His

190

mother was in the front row holding James. Her companions standing quietly on the side with the rest of the staff. The minister moved past him saying, "Pardon me Sam, I think I'll be more useful up front." Sam stood there staring until the minister's wife nudged him forward. "Are you going to make her wait any longer? or are you going to give her an anniversary date she can really celebrate?" Realizing what was going on Sam moved forward to take Anne's hand. They repeated the vows softly to each other and when the minister said, "You may now kiss the bride." Sam raised her veil and looked at her. She whispered. "I love you" and Sam caught his breath for a second before he sealed their wedding with a kiss that took her breath away. Everyone was laughing and clapping when they finally broke apart and Anne was blushing happily. Dinner was noisy with the children there, but Sam wouldn't have it any other way. April cheered when the cake was brought in and everyone laughed happily. When dinner was over, and the children taken upstairs to get ready for bed. The minister apologized for rambling on that afternoon. He and his wife were taken home by Adam. Then Anne turned to Sam. "Will you mind having to share your birthday with our anniversary every year darling?" Sam just shook his head in wonder. "What you said before, do you really mean it?" He asked hesitantly. Anne smiled. "Do I strike you as someone who doesn't mean what she says?" She asked. "I love you Sam. You've been wonderful to me and made my family our family. I want to grow old beside you. I want to raise however many children God gives us with you. I will never forget Donald. He was my first love and I will always miss him. You will too. But you are my last love." Hand in hand they walked upstairs to tuck in the children and read a story. When they got there Sam noticed that the cot Fiona slept on was gone from the corner. Anne saw his confusion and whispered, "The children are comfortable here. I don't think anyone has to stay in the room with them anymore. " Sam nodded and sat down to read. When the story was done, and prayers were said. Sam started to lead the way to the library as usual. Anne stopped him. "Wait Sam, I made some changes I want you to see. " She showed him a room with a single bed, desk and shelves in it. "I was thinking that Shawn should have his own room when he turns 10 next month. What do you think?" Sam looked around and replied. "That is a great idea. Let's have this be his practical present. We can put a globe and pens and paper on the desk. Perhaps hang a new outfit in the closet. There is room on the shelves for his tin army men and other toys that he won't want James to be getting into. It's a great idea. Perhaps the girls should have their own room as well when they get a bit older."

"Just what I had in mind." said Anne smiling. "The nursery might get a bit crowded." Sam hadn't been paying attention to where Anne was leading him. He looked at her a bit confused. "Won't James be lonely though?" Anne smiled, opened the door to his bedroom and said. "I certainly hope not." Sam stared at her for a moment and then scooped her up in his arms and entered the room kicking the door shut with his foot after they entered.

Chapter 12

Adventures with Eight

Jason was born almost exactly 9 months later. Grandmother was delighted to have more little ones around and often came to the nursery to rock him to sleep. Two years after that Lisa came along. Her middle name was Abigail and Grandmother had a hard time not spoiling her. The twins, Susan and Stephanie, followed 4 years later. 5 more years passed. The children were growing up. Shawn was almost 18. He had finished high school and was headed to college. Amy was 16 and had a long line of young men wanting to court her. She ignored most of them, preferring to read in the evening. She was considering nurses training in a couple years. April was 14 and no longer lisped. Sam missed that. She still asked questions about everything. When the newspaper grew from one page in another town's paper to a real weekly one of their own, she went to the editor and asked if they'd be interested in a column about school news. The editor told her in a very condescending tone that no one wanted to read about silly schoolgirl antics. April was furious and started a campaign at school to boycott the paper. She and her sister were very popular and managed to get many families to threaten to cancel the weekly paper if there wasn't school news in it written by one of the students. The editor capitulated but wanted to send a reporter to talk to the principal every week to get the news. Instead the principal came up with a contest. Every student who wanted could write an article for the paper. The editor would pick the one he wanted, and that student got the reporter job for the school year. The contest would be held every year during the first week of school. Faced with the united front the editor agreed. Two girls and one boy entered that first contest.

School News by the infamous Christine

This week at school we've been getting schedules, new books and meeting teachers. One of the girls who shall remain nameless wore a white dress the first day. Of course it wasn't white at the end of the day but she won't see the stain until she gets home! The new boy showed up still in knickers and was laughed out of the school. Everyone is excited that the new century starts soon. I'll report on that another time, right now I have to go see what everyone is giggling about over by my locker.

This week at school we have been getting acquainted with the new teachers and students. Our high school is growing every year. This year we will have a basketball team for the first time. One of the parents put up baskets on either side of the gym so they can practice during PE. We'll be publishing a schedule so everyone can come cheer on the team. Currently we don't have a name for the team but there have been many suggestions. The principal gets final say so. The players will be having an exhibition game to raise money for uniforms on September 23rd. Several parents have kindly agreed to put together a team to challenge them. Come out and cheer for your favorite team! Next week there is an all school meeting scheduled. The minister is coming to discuss how to treat classmates. His wife will talk to the girls. The staff is also putting together a dress code for regular school days and for gym class.

School News by Bart Billings the great.

We play basketball a lot. We're going to beat the parents team in a couple weeks so we can get uniforms to wear when we beat other teams. The minister is coming to tell us how to treat people. Guess it's because some scrawny kid showed up in knickers and we were honest with him. The Bible says not to lie so we probably did the right thing. Girls though they need that talk! They put red ink dots on that poor girls chair before she sat down. It was funny though. She walked around all day like that and never noticed. Bet she'll be in trouble when she gets home. After that the girls put a sign on one of the lockers in red that said "World's worst friend" Girls definitely need that talk.

April won and wrote an article every week until the end of the school year. She enjoyed writing and read her articles to Sam and Anne in the evening while Shawn studied, and Amy read. Her brother and sister encouraged her to keep writing even after school let out and Anne cut out and saved every article, pasting them in scrapbooks. James was 12 that year. He had grown up tall and strong. His favorite thing to do was still building things although he had graduated from blocks. One of the first real projects he did was to build a tree house. The girls clamored for one of their own, so he built them a small playhouse under a huge tree by the driveway. The younger children had taken them over. James didn't remember Donald or the years of poverty. It made him feel different sometimes and he never liked visiting the grave of his birth father. The first time he tried to refuse Anne and the girls cried and Sam and Shawn were furious. After a discussion on respect he never refused to go again. He didn't understand about saving money for a rainy day since he always could ask for more. Then one day Sam called him into the library and asked him to take on a project. Sam wanted a gazebo built in the flower garden. He would pay for it, but James had to figure out costs beforehand and present a plan. He would also pay James per hour to build it. James loved the idea and spent hours making sketches.

When he had one his mother liked he started
figuring costs. Instead of going to a lumber yard to
price the wood he estimated what it would cost. He
presented his plan to Sam who suggested he look
further into costs and that the paint be included since
his mother wanted it white. James just shrugged and
said, "There's plenty of paint in the shed and I'm
sure the lumber won't cost as much as you think."
After reminding him that costs over the estimate
came out of James wages, he approved the plan.
James got started that weekend. He asked Hunter to
help him take the wagon over to the lumber yard by
the river to pick up the wood. He was surprised to
find the lumber cost a bit more than he thought it
would but figured he'd just build a smaller gazebo.
That way it wouldn't take up as much of Gerald's
flowers. Hunter just smiled at that and helped him
load the wood. When they got home, and Sam found
out that the plans had changed he told James that the
gazebo had to be the size promised. James asked for
more money and Sam showed him the paper with
the estimate on it that said final cost. Frowning
James went to complain to Shawn. His big brother
sided with Papa but suggested that there were a lot
of trees in the woods free for taking. Maybe he
could work out a deal with the lumber yard owner
for trees in exchange for boards. James thanked him
and ran to telephone the lumber yard. The owner

agreed to take trees in exchange for boards but
reminded James that while each tree might make
several boards it took a great deal of work to mill it
down. They agreed that two boards per tree would
be a fair exchange. James went in search of his Papa
to ask him to have the trees chopped down and
hauled to the yard. Sam agreed that he could have
ten trees for the boards he needed free of cost but
told him he either had to pay someone to chop them
or chop them himself. The lumber yard was coming
to pick them up in two weeks. James decided to
chop them down himself and spent every day after
school and every night after dinner chopping. He
was exhausted and his schoolwork was suffering.
His friend stopped coming around because he was
too busy to talk to them other than at lunch. The
evening before the lumber yard was due to pick
them up, he finished. Anne was so relieved. She
understood the lesson Sam was trying to teach her
son but seeing him that tired every day was hard on
her. Sam watched out the library window every
night for hours praying for James to have strength
and be safe as well as for their relationship which
was a bit strained. The yard delivered the boards
when they picked up the trees and James set to
work. He sawed the boards into the size pieces he
needed and then set off to the shed to get the nail
barrel. It wasn't there so he went looking for Gerald

to see if it was moved. "No Lad, I didn't move it.
Perhaps it was empty. Besides, a construction
contractor doesn't use other people's nails, they buy
their own." James groaned when he heard that. He
walked to the store adding up the number of nails as
he went. Since he had been so busy cutting trees, he
hadn't spent his pocket money from the last two
weeks. He bought as many nails as he could and
trudged home hoping for a loaves and fishes event
on the nails. The next day James got up early and
got right to work. It was Saturday so he could spend
the whole day pounding nails. He was half done.
Sunday was church and family time so he couldn't
work that day. Monday after school he ran out of
nails. Luckily Sam had left their weekly pocket
money by their places that morning before he left for
work. James bought more nails Tuesday after
school. Thursday, he finished building the gazebo.
As he stood there proudly Anne walked up behind
him and placed her arm across his shoulders. "Oh
honey, it looks beautiful! I can't wait to see it
painted!" "Painted" replied James slowly. "Yes,
well it looks like it might rain so I might not get it
painted until next week." Anne looked confused
since the sky was clear, but she just smiled and
nodded. Sam came to see it later that night and
offered to advance the money for paint against his
pay for building it. James gratefully accepted and

brought paint home after school the next day. By Saturday the gazebo was finished, and James proudly led his family out to see it. As everyone stood admiring his work, he realized that Lisa had picked up a bent nail and was trying to write on a piece of scrap wood. Before he could stop her, she started to cry. Everyone reached for her, but he got there first. She had pricked her finger with the nail. He picked her up and wrapped his handkerchief around the wound. Sam and Anne handed the twins to the girls and joined him. Sam grabbed the nail and was examining it for rust and soil while Anne took Lisa up to the house to thoroughly wash the cut. Everyone but Sam and James trailed after her. James looked up at Sam terrified. "She won't get tetanus will she Papa? I'm sorry I didn't clean the site. I never thought about it. I'll clean it right now." Sam just shook his head. "I don't know son all we can do is pray. I appreciate your offer to clean up. When your done come to the library and we'll settle up." When the area around the gazebo was spotless James ran to the house. He didn't go to the library to collect his pay though. Instead he went to the nursery to check on his little sister. He told her how sorry he was that she got cut and then sat down and played with the dollhouse with her until dinner time. When Fiona came in to settle the younger ones for dinner he offered to stay and help serve the kids for her. Shawn came looking for him when he didn't show up to the table. He reported back that James wasn't hungry and would be staying in the nursery that evening. Sam and Anne were worried about Lisa too, so they understood. When it came time to tuck the younger ones into bed, they insisted James come down to the library with them for family devotions. Everyone prayed Lisa would be fine. After the others drifted off Sam sat with James to show him the original estimate and costs for the gazebo. He praised him for using his own money to buy what he needed and for cutting down trees to come up with the extra wood. James said he had learned his lesson and would never turn in an estimate without all the stuff needed for the structure priced correctly. Hesitantly he asked if he had earned any money over what the paint cost. "Yes" said Sam "But maybe not much more than the pocket money you paid out." He handed him 2 dollars. James stared at the money for a moment. He looked up at Papa and then threw himself into his arms. "What if Lisa gets sick? What if she dies because of my carelessness? I didn't think about the little bits on the ground" "Easy James." Soothed Sam. "Your mother and I were there too. We share in the responsibility. As soon as we got there, we knew there were hazards. You don't have to take all this alone. They prayed for Lisa together and then

James hugged his Papa and thanked him for the lesson. He headed upstairs to bed and Anne came in. Her face had worry lines and Sam reached for her. They prayed together for their little girl and for James. That night there was a knock on their door about 3 A.M. Jumping up they opened the door to see Fiona. Fearing the worst, they ran for the nursery not giving her a chance to explain why she had awakened them. When they got there, they found James curled up on the rug below Lisa's bed sound asleep. Lisa was fine. They had a couple weeks to wait to be sure they were safe but for now their baby slept quietly. After a whispered conversation with Fiona where she explained that she had been awakened by a noise and went in to find James sleeping on the floor. Thanking her for letting them know they told her to get some sleep. They decided to let James stay there. After school the next day James stopped at the store. He brought home bubble gum for Lisa. James spoiled her until Anne finally put a stop to it. She declared the child healthy and made James stay in his own bed and forbid him to buy her any more candy. The next day Lisa came down to the library and told her parents that her jaw hurt. It was swollen on the left side as well. Instant deep fear leapt into their hearts. It took a great deal to not scare the child. Sam sat her on his lap and asked her to open her mouth. When she closed it, he asked how long her jaw had been hurting. "Ever since I put the other piece of bubble gum in my mouth" she replied. Sam handed her a rag to spit the gum into. He cuddled her for a bit and then asked how her jaw felt. "Fine" she said. "I'm all better." Relieved Anne asked where she had gotten the gum. "I saved it from when James gave me some firstist." She lisped. Sam hugged her and sent her off to play. "Let's hope that's the end of the gum." Whispered Anne. "I don't think I could take any more moments like that!" Then she looked more closely at Sam. "Oh, go ahead and laugh! I'll laugh with you someday I'm sure!" Sam burst out laughing at her expression and Anne started to smile. "I'm asking Fiona to check for other hiding places tomorrow though, just in case!" Life continued to be exciting and fun for the King family. They had their hands full with little ones getting into everything and older ones starting to date. Fiona was being courted by a nice young man who worked in the mines and Sam and Anne were worried she'd leave. One evening she came to them and asked if she could talk to them. Sam and Anne clasped hands and sat to listen. Fiona led with "I'm engaged." Anne stood up and hugged her and Sam offered their congratulations. Fiona had tears in her eyes though and Sam asked if there was more, she had to tell them. "I don't want to leave." She cried. I've been here since I was 16 and I love your children. I don't know what to do." Sam gave a sigh of relief. "We don't want you to either. How about you continue to live here with your husband?" We can make up a suite for you or build a cabin on the property for you. Whichever you'd prefer." Freya looked up excitedly. "Really? You'd do that for me?" Anne smiled. "We'd be doing it for us Freya!" I'd love to have you stay and when the time comes, your babies can share the nursery. You talk to your young man and find out what he'd prefer. If it's a cabin, we'll raise your salary since you won't be eating all your meals here. If you want to live in the house, he can eat here too. Perhaps he'd like to help out occasionally to cover that cost." Freya laughed, I'm pretty sure he'll want to live here. You see I can't cook. I can't even boil water. I went to make tea once and burned the pan." Relieved they chatted a bit more about the children's antics and then Fiona went to bed. Sam and Anne stayed up talking about the changes they'd seen over the last 10 years. The country had changed quite a lot and the family as well. In a couple months it would be a new century. The coal mine was getting played out. Coal wouldn't last more than another few years and Sam was desperately trying to find an industry he could start in Hope that would keep everyone employed. Financially they were set for many more generations, but he worried about the miners, especially the ones who had no other skills. He needed to find a way of propelling Hope into the Industrial Revolution that was sweeping America. He decided to steer clear of other fossil fuels since they too could run out. Instead he looked into producing steel, but it was too expensive to transport iron ore from the Midwest and besides, Pittsburgh was becoming the leader and he didn't feel they could compete. He wanted to get into the railroad industry in some way but didn't feel they had the resources to make the actual cars as well as they did in Chicago. Finally, he decided to start two different industries, toys and electronics. He figured he'd keep which ever seemed most profitable. He built two factories and hired two experts to come in and advise him. At the next meeting with the miners he explained that no one would be forced to leave the mines, but he needed workers for the factories. Pay would be similar but shifts would be different. He offered retraining to anyone who wanted it. Most of the younger miners took him up on his offer. The miners who were looking at retirement decided to stay in the mines until they couldn't find any more coal. At the end of the meeting it was decided to close two of the shafts. They might be reopened if the other two failed. Sam also cut the hours to only two shifts. Everyone could be home to sleep at

night. As usual the union representative complained but the men shouted him down and threatened to withdraw from the union. The representative admitted that it was a better outcome than he'd expected when he came to the meeting. A lot of mines were being shut down with no jobs provided by their employer and retraining while offered by the United Mine Workers wasn't as effective as they had hoped. Sam and Anne were satisfied that between the new industries and the changes in the mine, Hope was protected from becoming a ghost town.